SAVE THE
LAST DANCE

SAVE THE LAST DANCE

•

Marie Sparks

AVALON BOOKS
NEW YORK

PRINTED IN THE UNITED STATES OF AMERICA
ON ACID-FREE PAPER
BY HADDON CRAFTSMEN, BLOOMSBURG, PENNSYLVANIA

I wish to dedicate this novel to Christine, Howie, Brent, and Jennifer, my much loved and always helpful cheering section.

Chapter One

Marla Shelton looked up from where she stood grooming her mustang mare, met Jace Van Garrett's incredible gaze, and immediately lost her voice. His eyes were a striking hazel with cat-green flecks and brown highlights. Funny, she didn't remember them being so vivid. He reached out, playfully pulled her off her feet and up into his arms, then swung her around as though she was a child.

Marla pushed against his muscular chest with all her might. "Put me down, Jace," she sputtered. "What do you think you're doing?"

"Whoa . . ." he said with a chuckle, and placed a finger against Marla's lips, smiling all the while. "Don't be so all-fired wiggly." His deep voice brimmed with male sensuality as he set her down. "Darn, if you haven't grown up since the last time I saw you, sunshine. Pretty, too." His eyes traveled her length, and his expression heated, telling her he liked what he saw, secretly flattering her.

"Oh, you . . . you . . ." she muttered, tucking in her shirt while trying to regain her composure.

Jace broke into a grin, the scar at the corner of his eye dancing in the tiny folds of skin. "Does that mean we're not sweethearts?"

Marla shook her head, exasperation rising to her face. "You got that right, mister know-it-all. We've never been sweethearts and never will be, for that matter." She neglected to mention the enormous crush she'd once had on him even though he was much older than her—all of five years.

"Never is a long time," he said, drawing out the words.

Marla picked up the currycomb she'd been using on the horse and tossed it dangerously near his booted toe. He whistled, and with an ease of motion, bent to sweep up the comb in his large hand. "Hey, I was expecting to see a gal with painful looking braces on her teeth and her blond hair in pigtails. You've gone and surprised the heck out of me."

"I haven't had braces since I was fourteen," she said with righteous pride. "A few years can make a whole lot of difference, you dimwit. As for you, you look even more dog-eared than the last time I saw you." A lie. She let her own glance slide boldly over him.

Everyone around knew Jace Van Garrett was a ruggedly handsome hunk. His dark brown hair curled at his collar and his level eyes made you think he was looking straight through to your soul. But Marla had no intention of adding herself to the succession of young women eager to land him for a husband.

Jace slapped his broad-brimmed hat against his knee. "I didn't know your irises were the color of violets," he said, smoothing his tongue across his lips, a hint of amusement etched around the corners of his mouth. He gave her the old Jace smile she remembered so well, but she didn't let herself respond to his attempt at charm.

Marla flipped back her thick hair and gave him a dismissive wave of the hand, raising her chin with disapproval. "You still have the manners of a frog."

A long moment of silence followed as his grin faded. She felt a moment of satisfaction mixed with guilt. He seemed taller and his face had taken on more character lines now that he was inching toward thirty. Tautly muscled, there had always been a restlessness about him that appealed to her.

That morning Marla's mother had casually mentioned he hadn't yet put a ring on some woman's finger. He'd most likely scared them off with his brash behavior, Marla thought contemptuously, though she knew it wasn't true. He could get pretty near any woman in the valley he wanted. Except her. Darn it, now she was even lying to herself.

"Heard about your father's accident. Real sorry," Jace said. "How's he doing?"

Marla felt a lump rise in the back of her throat. She'd been so happy living in Flagstaff and preparing for a teaching career in the fall, but that was before she'd been called home. Her father couldn't have prevented what happened, yet the resentment she harbored added to her burden.

"Thanks for asking. Dad broke his leg in two places.

It was pretty bad, and he's got metal pins in him now. Boy, does he hate being in the hospital."

"I'll bet."

"I'm looking after things around here."

"I heard. I also heard you didn't like my idea regarding those mules. What's the problem?" he asked. "The drought's getting worse, not better. They'll die out there if they don't get aid."

"How could I possibly agree with you?" she asked and raised her chin. "Your idea's all wrong."

He crossed his arms over the breadth of his wide chest. "Better fed than dead. Seriously, trying to come to an amicable agreement can sometimes be harder than plucking clay pigeons. But time isn't something we have a lot of." Towering over her, he reached to smooth the furrow between her eyebrows with his thumb. "Those angry lines might get stuck there permanently, like a woodpecker's rat-a-tat on a tree," he said.

"You think you're so clever," she fumed. "Go away before I turn the hose on you."

Jace put his hands up as though to shield his face and gave her a big grin. The mare nickered and shook her silky mane as though she agreed, causing Jace to laugh. "Smart horse," he said.

Marla couldn't keep a laugh from escaping, too. "Naturally, I trained her," she said.

Jace leaned back on his heels, slipped a hand in the pocket of his tight blue jeans, and removed a piece of carrot. He held it to the horse's mouth and watched her gobble the veggie, then he swung his attention back to Marla. "You going to the meeting at the firehouse this afternoon?"

"Count on it."

"Don't keep Patterson waiting. Government types hate being inconvenienced. The dude'll be anxious to take the first flight back to civilization."

Jace plopped his cowboy hat back on his head and tipped it politely. "I'm off like a herd of desert turtles," he said, pulling a grin, then spun on his heel and headed for the paint-peeled, dusty pickup truck he'd driven over to the ranch.

Seeing him had taken Marla completely by surprise. She'd been away from the valley for several years working her way through college in Flagstaff. Jace might still think of her as the kid on the neighboring ranch, but that was about to change. He'd soon learn she'd become a woman to be reckoned with.

Marla shielded her eyes from the sun and watched Jace rev up the pickup's engine. It purred like a kitten as he headed down the rutted road, a fine mist of dust trailing. She gritted her teeth, hoping he had gotten the message. There'd be no more teasing, thank you.

Marla thought about the schism brewing. If Jace thought she'd let the free-roaming mules be sold to ranchers, he could think again. Until the devastating drought hit the valley, there'd never been a problem. However, attitudes changed fast, and the ranchers were grousing about the wild herd.

Bettina, her mustang mare, swished her tail to discourage a pesky fly as Marla picked up the lead rope and sauntered back to the stables. To Marla's thinking, nothing wild should be domesticated. Sure, she'd tamed Bettina, but that was different. The mare had been a sickly foal and if left on her own would have become red meat for the mountain lions and coyotes in the hills surrounding the valley. She couldn't let that happen.

Jace Van Garrett's ideas about what was best for the mules was wrong from the get-go. Would the agent from the Bureau of Land Management side with him? This troubling thought had caused her several sleepless nights. No one knew how the mules got there, though some folks said they had been dumped by an itinerant traveling rodeo.

The drought continued to devastate the region. People couldn't water their lawns or wash cars. Many were driving all the way to Flagstaff to do laundry in coin operated laundromats. Showers were necessarily of short duration, and everyone was buying bottled water with fresh water earmarked for livestock.

The Shelton horse ranch bordered the Van Garrett cattle ranch near the small town of Coyote Springs, Arizona, fifty miles from Flagstaff. Marla would be meeting Jace and the bureau agent at the city fire department. She showered, put on clean jeans and a yellow cotton blouse, added lipstick and blush, something she seldom wore, then ran a brush through her hair before hurrying downstairs.

Marla's aging, one-eyed tomcat was sleeping in the Jeep Cherokee when she came outside. She picked Sugar from the seat and nuzzled him affectionately before placing him on the ground. He had a habit of jumping through the rolled down truck windows and taking advantage of the soft cushions, leaving cat hair and paw marks behind.

"I'll be back, Sugar," she murmured, and closed the

truck door. The cat strolled away, its scroungy tail raised in a haughty manner.

On the way to Coyote Springs, Marla drove through a pass with rock formations as high as the roof of a two-story house. Beyond, a sudden wailing wind blew down from the mountain range and swept across the dead grassland, hurling a tumbleweed against the front of the Jeep. Trees undulated like go-go dancers and dust circles swirled across the road.

The wind gradually died away as Marla reached the outskirts of town. She drove down the main street and glanced toward the small school on the left, its windows boarded up. Officially closed, the bleak picture gave her a sad feeling in the pit of her stomach. She'd wanted to teach there.

The district had lost its only teacher and become a victim of cost cutting. Marla thought it was a shame folks around wouldn't be seeing the flag flying over the building and kids playing in the yard come September. The children would be bussed back and forth to Flagstaff, making for a very long day. So much for economizing.

The firehouse parking lot lay ahead. Marla flipped on her turn signal and pulled in, unfastened the seat belt, and got out. She'd heard Jace was the new volunteer fire chief, as though he didn't have enough to do on his spread. But ask a busy person . . . as the old saying went.

Marla slipped her sunglasses into a pocket of her leather purse and glanced up at the big door that had been rolled up to the ceiling. The bright red fire engine inside the building hovered as though ready to sprint into action. She took a moment to look at a framed drawing on a wall, a caricature of a Dalmatian with a smily face and a gold tooth.

"We're in here," Jace called to Marla as her boots tapped on the cement floor, announcing her arrival. He held a door open for her. "You made it, and on time. Just great."

She strolled past him, whispering loud enough for him to hear, "What did you expect?"

After the introductions, Marla reluctantly took a seat beside Jace. So they'd already been talking before she arrived. Uncool. She considered Jace over-the-top traitorous and wasn't looking forward to this meeting of minds. He laid his hat on the floor between them and accidentally brushed the back of his hand along her knee. Her heart did a double beat, and she stabbed him with a glare. If he wanted to keep her off-balance, it wouldn't work. Concentrating on the agent, she sat up straight in the chair, and ignored Jace.

The bureau agent, Harold Patterson, occupied the metal office desk. He spent the next moments cleaning his glasses. A garland of thin gray hair and a sunburned pate didn't add dignity to the man. Like someone with a permanent scowl, he frowned from behind the tinted bifocal glasses he'd shoved onto the bridge of his splayed nose. "Let's get down to business," he said.

"Right," Jace Van Garrett said. "I'm very concerned about those mules."

And she wasn't? Marla gave Jace a hard sidelong glance. His strong profile made him look very determined. He extended his long legs to the side away from her and sat at an uncomfortable angle.

Patterson fingered a thick portfolio on the desktop.

"You received my letters concerning the mules, I take it?" he asked with a world-weary air.

Marla and Jace responded with nods. She sized Agent Patterson up as a soft-bellied man with a bureaucrat's lack of interest. Passionate about the mules' survival, she perched on the edge of the chair, ready to put in her two cents.

The agent cleared his throat. "It's urgent that something be done about the mules. The bureau has gotten complaints from ranchers who say the mules descend on them like a herd of locusts, eat up hay and exploit their water reserves. I don't mind telling you it's one big headache. As for the environmentalists, they're complaining too. Don't want the mules touched. But that's nothing new." He pursed his mouth. "Since your families control the largest acreage in the valley, I want your input before taking any action."

His eyes slid from Jace to Marla then back to Jace. She held her breath, not liking the "let us ol' boys stick together" look on his face. "I understand, Mr. Van Garrett, that you think they should be sold to ranchers," the agent said. Jace opened his mouth to speak but Agent Patterson switched back to Marla. "However, you're against that suggestion, Ms. Shelton. Am I correct?"

Marla gave him a quick shake of her head. "I think we should ship them away to grasslands in Montana or Wyoming until the water situation improves around here."

Agent Patterson's thin lips twitched, clueing Marla in on the man's probable decision, and it didn't look favorable to her. "That's expensive," he muttered. "Besides, I'm told the grass is drying up and the water supply is low up there, as well."

Marla realized she'd been holding her breath, then let her next words pour out on the expelled air. "Surely there are other places, sir. The mules have grown wild. Everyone with any sense knows that, and I don't think you'd find many people who'd want to buy them. They eat up landscaping like goats and would probably keep the horses in a stew."

The agent gave it some thought. "Well, a resolution must be made before the ranchers commence to shooting them."

Marla leaped to her feet. "Over my dead body!" she snapped. Things weren't going the way she wanted and she racked her brain trying to come up with a solution.

Agent Patterson's mouth dropped open and he stared at Marla over his glasses. Marla took her seat, figuring she may have gone a trifle overboard with the dramatics. "This valley has always been a sanctuary for the herd," she said in a calmer voice. "We could send them away on a temporary basis, then bring them back after the rains replenish the land. It's the only reasonable thing to do."

The agent sighed heavily and folded his hands, palms down, on the official-looking papers. "I seriously doubt the government will go to the expense of transplanting the herd. It's not like they're mustangs. And you must realize belt-tightening's going on in Washington as we speak."

Jace lifted a dark eyebrow and let his gaze settle on Marla. "I never suggested the mules be sold," he said in a strained voice. "We could divide them up. It's less of a hit on each rancher that way. Give them to good homes, to people who'd care for them. And yes, train those mules to do something beneficial. They'd make fine pack animals, for one. You talk as though that's a hideous crime, Marla. Be practical, for God's sake. We're not living in some utopia."

She bristled. "I'd rather see the herd rounded up and shipped away somewhere," she insisted. "How about Colorado?"

Jace grimaced but kept his voice well modulated. "Even if the bureau agreed to send them elsewhere, we'd probably never see them again," he told Marla. Then he turned to Patterson. "Over the years, the mules have become such a fixture here in the valley, like pet geese for example, that we want to see them protected."

Marla interrupted. "Maybe it wouldn't hurt to wait out the drought a little longer," she reasoned. "It'll soon be monsoon weather. If worse comes to worst, we could donate enough hay from neighboring ranches to stave off hunger until the rains. My family, for one, would be willing to share."

Jace shook his head. "You're being short-sighted. We'll all be lucky if we can feed our own livestock. And what about water? The water table has dropped drastically. As for the monsoon, there's no guarantee it will even come this year."

Ignoring his remark, Marla threw out a question. "How do you know those mules would go to good homes? I've heard tales of people selling mustangs to dog food factories in Mexico. They might do the same with the mules."

"That just isn't going to happen," Jace shot back, his hazel eyes darkening.

Marla gave him a quizzical look. "How do you know?"

"Because it's an old rumor and rumors like that fly around all the time. More often than not, with no substance."

Agent Patterson scratched his ear. "It appears we aren't getting anywhere." He pushed back his chair and lumbered to his feet. "Tell you what. I'll give you forty-eight hours to come to an agreement. If you don't, then I'll make the decision. Give me a call when you're ready, folks."

He handed them official business cards and reached across the desk to shake their hands, then picked up his attaché case and strode from the office.

Left alone, Jace and Marla stared warily at one another, his mouth etched with discontent. She was determined not to be bested by this stubborn man.

For once Jace wasn't giving Marla one of those silly grins and acting like she was a kid. Just maybe he realized now she'd actually grown up and that he'd met his match. She considered going after Agent Patterson and resuming her argument, but thought better of it. Well, this meant she'd have to meet with Jace again, as well as get busy on the telephone drumming up support among the ranchers. Marla wasn't ready to concede anything.

Chapter Two

The alarm clock beeped three times and Marla got up, shutting off the annoying racket. She opened the window and breathed in fresh air to sweep away the cobwebs from her brain. A ring of sunlit gold surrounded the valley. She pulled on a pair of faded blue jeans and then scoured the chest of drawers looking for a shirt to wear. She removed a lavender tank top and tossed it over her head. Her favorite boots lent the finishing touch. Thoughts of being unable to teach this fall slipped back into her consciousness like a damp rag, bringing on a sense of sadness. Why did life have to be so complicated? When she'd applied to the Flagstaff school district, she'd practically been guaranteed a position. Then her father had had his accident and she'd decided to put the job on hold. What else could she do? Her parents needed her. Still, she found herself in the doldrums over the missed opportunity.

Marla hurried downstairs, took a bowl from the

kitchen cupboard, poured milk from the fridge, and ate an uninteresting mishmash of cold cereals. Her mother, devoted to her husband, had already left for the hospital. Marla had visited him the previous night, just before Jace Van Garrett called. Her father hadn't been in the best mood but what had she expected?

With a muffled sigh, Marla tried to look at the good side. At least it was only Charlie's leg that was broken. Better than his neck. That reasoning helped a little, making her determined to get into a more positive frame of mind before she started her work day. JoAnn, her mother, always said negative vibes could spread like poison.

Marla rinsed the things she'd used, put them in the dishwasher, picked up an apple from the fruit bowl on the table, then strolled outside, closing the screen door behind her. A bay colt in the corral across the barnyard whinnied. He was a frisky beauty, bursting with energy. She sauntered up to the fence just as he ran toward her full tilt, his tail hoisted like a flag. Then he came to a shuddering halt and stretched his long, graceful neck over the fence rail.

"Major, you're a big beggar," Marla said with affection. "I know exactly what you want." She showed the yearling the apple. His eyes glowed and he shook his head, his mane rippling in the breeze.

Marla offered the apple to him, her palm open. He removed the fruit with his lips and munched noisily. She chuckled. How could anyone stay depressed around such a spirited animal? He made her feel like everything would be okay.

Marla walked on to the stable in a better mood and

saddled her mustang mare. Impatient for a gallop, Bettina stamped one hoof. "I'm just as eager as you are," she told the horse. Bettina's ears flicked forward. "I wonder where the heck those mules have gone to." With any luck, Marla would catch a glimpse of them today.

Hearing someone humming, Marla glanced over to see Jeff Begay, their Navajo ranch hand, busily mucking out a stall at the far end of the stables.

"Hey, Jeff. I didn't see you," she called. He tipped his straw hat to her. "I'll be back in a couple of hours. Then we can work with the colt."

"Sure thing," Jeff said, an eager look on his square face. A sturdy young man of twenty, he had straight black hair and high cheekbones. Completely in love with everything about horses, he was very responsible and wanted to be a trainer. Marla realized how fortunate they were to have Jeff on the ranch at this time.

"How's your dad coming along?" he asked. "That sassy calf managed to twist Charlie's leg into a pretzel when he tried to brand it."

"Dad's looking at months before the fractures heal," she said. "Thanks for working overtime."

"No problem." He put down the big fork and sauntered over to her, wiping his hands on his jeans.

She hesitated before going on. "Jeff, I hired a horse trainer from Florida. It seemed the only sensible thing to do seeing as how that Wyoming rancher wants a dozen of the cutting horses by the first of October."

A muscle in Jeff's jaw worked and he looked disappointed, though he tried to hide it by lowering the brim of his hat. "I see," he said in an even voice. "When's he coming?"

"In a few days. You'll need to show him the ropes since Jace Van Garrett and I will probably go on a roundup to bring those wild mules in." She shook her head. "Having that big job thrown at me couldn't have come at a worse time."

Jeff shifted his stance. "No kidding?" Before she could reply, his mouth formed a question. "Say you catch 'em, then what will you do? Oh, I heard they can be more ornery than rodeo bulls."

"The agent from the bureau asked Jace and I to come up with a plan."

"Like what?"

She shrugged her shoulders. "That's one big problem. We can't seem to agree." She quickly explained their differences.

"Hmm," was all Jeff said. He reached up and held the mustang's bridle for Marla to mount. She took the reins, slipped her booted foot in the stirrup, swung into the saddle, and gave Jeff a thank you smile as he released the horse.

"See you around, Jeff." Marla said, then turned her attention to the mare. "Let's go, girl. Maybe we'll find a grassy location for those freeloading relatives of yours." The mare twitched a veined ear and nickered as though she understood, causing Marla to laugh. It felt good to be in the saddle.

Marla rode through the grove of cottonwood trees circling the perimeter of the horse ranch. Bettina's hoofs clip-clopped on the hard-packed earth. The sun warmed Marla's back as she turned west and let the miles distance her from her home.

After a while, she reined in to let the mare rest in the

shade of a pinon tree. Gnarled oaks and golden grass spread out ahead of her. She removed her straw hat and fanned the beads of perspiration on her forehead, recalling what Agent Patterson had said the day before about the mules. The agent hadn't given them much time to come to a decision.

Racking her brain for a reasonable alternative, Marla gazed as far as she could see across the dry valley. If only she could locate suitable grazing land at a higher elevation, yet she knew it was probably an impossibility, though she had to try.

Thunderheads loomed over the mountain range, clouds that refused to drop a speck of rain. Was Jace right? She thought about his phone call last night asking if she'd changed her mind. Oh, he could be persuasive, that one. He'd said he understood how she felt, and that her ideas held merit, but that the man from the bureau had already told them the government wouldn't foot the bill for transfering the mules. She'd argued that maybe they could find grazing land somewhere. He hadn't scoffed but he might just as well have.

All at once Marla heard leather creaking and a horse's grunt. She twisted in the saddle and saw Jace's steady approach over an incline. Had he been following her? She wasn't a believer in coincidences.

Jace caught up to Marla, leaned his big frame back in the saddle, and said, "Hey there, sunshine. You're out early."

She tossed him a vague smile. "What are you doing here?"

"Great day for a ride," he said, not giving her an answer. He took off his broad-brimmed hat and combed his fingers through his dark hair. "We'll need to contact Patterson soon, and we can't very well discuss things if you run off by yourself."

"I didn't run off," Marla said with a sarcastic tinge in her voice. She deliberately shifted her attention to his gray gelding. "Big horse. He must be all of seventeen hands high."

"Just about. Gun Powder and I needed some exercise so I came by your place to have that talk Patterson suggested. Jeff said you'd ridden off somewhere. I took a chance you'd head in this direction." He reached out to untangle the gelding's mane. His plaid shirt, with its sleeves cut out, exposed tanned, sinewy arms.

Marla adjusted her sunglasses. "I thought I'd take a look around. You know, ride into the hill country and see if I could find grass."

He looked at her like he doubted her sanity. "Really." However, the timbre of his voice changed. "I'm sorry we couldn't come to an agreement. This is serious business, though. Heaven only knows what Patterson will do with the herd if we don't."

Marla wet her lower lip with the tip of her tongue before speaking. "I thought about that, too." She couldn't help notice the swirl of dark chest hair peeking over the top button of Jace's shirt, but quickly drew her attention to his face.

A sudden flurry whipped a tendril of Marla's hair against her cheek. With one swift movement, Jace tucked the strand behind her ear. The sensation of his fingers against her skin caused her to swallow hard and glance away, her heart thumping overtime.

"Nice out here," he said, letting his attention sweep toward the hills.

"Yeah." It somehow seemed less lonely now that Jace was here. Marla noted the change in him. Not quite so cocky today. She studied a butte in the distance as though she'd never seen it before. "Looks like one of those paintings you see for sale in galleries in Sedona and Flagstaff," she said, making conversation to still her heart.

He nodded easily. "Yeah. Before Mom's accident, she used to paint scenes like that, and she was pretty darn good."

"I remember," Marla said. JoAnn Shelton and Mary Van Garrett had been the best of friends since girlhood. Mary, however, had suffered some devastating blows along the way, like her husband dying of a heart attack, and then her going blind. In one respect, she was lucky, and that was having a son like Jace to take over the running of the family cattle ranch. It meant Mary could stay on the land she loved and wouldn't have to sell the place. Her daughter Debra had recently moved back to the valley, too. She and Marla were good friends.

Marla's mare impatiently shifted her stance and Marla patted the horse on the withers to settle her. "Guess I'll be moving on," she announced to Jace, then laid the reins to the side of the horse's neck. "You coming?"

Jace's face lightened. "Thought you'd never ask."

The horses moved onto a wide, well-used trail. Marla knew Jace was about busting his buttons to discuss the mule problem. Finally, he blurted, "Let's stop pussy-footing around. Nothing's going to get settled with our wandering the countryside like Sunday drivers. If we're going to round up the herd, we ought to be on the trail in a day or two." There was no trace of smugness in his voice.

Marla adjusted her hat. "I wasn't evading the issue," she said, tossing him a challenge. "Well, go on. Say what you're going to."

Face set into a serious mold, Jace pointed to the west. "Let's head toward that mesa first. If the stream isn't dried up, we can let the horses drink."

Irritated that he chose not to talk about the mules at that moment, she followed him. "We might even find some green grass," she said stoutly.

He cracked a grin. "Don't hold your breath."

All at once, the horses bumped into one another. The mare reached around and tried to take a nip out of the gelding's long neck. Marla and Jace shared a chuckle.

"Aggressive little lady," he said.

"She's got an independent nature," Marla said. "It's in her mustang blood."

Jace admired the rhythmic way Marla's trim body swayed in the saddle as they moved on. "You're a born horsewoman," he said.

Marla scarcely reacted. He had watched her grow up and remembered well the fiery, determined girl who'd joined the wranglers on many roundups. Everyone in the valley knew she was an expert horse trainer too. But that wasn't all. She'd also worked in the alfalfa fields alongside the hired hands and wasn't shy about taking on just about any project.

Jace had always liked the spunky tomboy. Yet seeing Marla as a full-fledged woman had about blown his mind, making him unsure as to how to approach her. Well, he hadn't handled it well. What a fiasco! He'd twirled her around and got a scolding with a capital 'S'.

They reached the mesa and found the stream. "Pitiful," Jace said as he stood looking down at the scarce water. He reached for Marla, who sat astride her horse. "Let me give you a hand, sunshine," he said.

The moment his hands circled Marla's narrow waist he experienced a throbbing beat in his chest, followed by a heightened awareness of her femininity. Marla's beautifully shaped lips were only a kiss away from his.

However, with a barrel full of reluctance, he averted his gaze and set her down. They let the horses drink before tethering them, then found a shady spot. He dropped down on the beige grass beside her.

"You were gone from the valley for a long time," Jace reflected. "Tell me about college." He wanted to ease his way back into the matter of the mules without antagonizing her, thinking it best to start the conversation on a less prickly topic.

Marla brought her knees up and cupped them with her arms, a smile blooming on her pretty face. "I graduated last year and worked two more semesters practice teaching in order to get my credential."

"What was your major?"

"English. I'd hoped to move to Flagstaff and teach, though with Dad laid up, I'll have to decline if the offer comes through."

"Sorry. It must mean a lot to you," Jace said. He felt like he'd gotten a gut-punch when she mentioned wanting to move away again.

"You're right, it does mean a lot to me." She sighed. "I love it here in the valley but sometimes a person has to make hard choices," she said. "I want to teach and that means leaving here."

Jace heard the pain in her voice, pain she was valiantly trying to hide. He thought about the local school having closed and frustration built inside him. "You could have taught in Coyote Springs if circumstances were different."

"That's what I'd originally intended to do," she said.

A seed of an idea took root in the back of his mind. What if the school could somehow be reopened in the fall? Nah. It wasn't going to happen.

Jace let his gaze roam freely over Marla. She was an attractive, small-boned woman, about five feet two, if he guessed right, and it amazed him how her slender hands could control a capricious horse. But then he knew from experience she had a gentle touch with animals and they seemed to respond to the empathy she had for them. Her thick, dark blond hair shimmered in waves that put him in mind of a lake just before the sun goes down. Her eyes were a startling blue and could change to indigo when she grew angry, a phenomenon that fascinated him.

Marla smiled and he returned the smile, realizing he was only now beginning to know Marla, the woman. Like a gazelle, she swiftly shifted the subject. "I want the mules to survive, Jace. More than anything," she said in a passion-filled voice. "They were tossed away like castoffs but managed to adapt and make a home for themselves here on the range. They deserve to live out their days in peace."

Normally Jace would have agreed with her, but drastic

changes were needed to save the animals. "Hunger and thirst will weaken the herd, make them easy prey to predators. Mountain lions and coyotes are probably already dogging their trail."

Marla grimaced. "We can't let that happen."

Jace tossed her a studied look. "The question gets back to how, doesn't it?"

She let out her breath. "I caught sight of them last Christmas when I came home for the holidays. Gosh, but they're smart. If people only knew."

The enthusiasm in Marla's remarks reminded Jace of when she was, what—fifteen? They'd held a barbecue on his ranch and her family had come. She'd buttonholed him, letting the words fly out of her mouth about a yearling her father had purchased. "I'll make Prince into the best cutting horse around. You'll see," she'd said, her eyes glittering like exquisite aquamarines. She liked to name the horses noble names, nothing common like Bill or Sal or Ol' Lop Ears. They had to be called Princess or King or Robin Hood.

The recollection wrapped around Jace's heart. Had that been the day he'd fallen in love with her, knowing it would be a long while until she grew up? Well, he was a patient man and she was worth the wait. But she'd made other plans before he'd even heard about it and left for college. Somehow, in his busy life, he'd nearly lost track of her. Now she was home and he'd held her briefly in his arms. The surprised look in her eyes had nearly undone him, and she'd sputtered like a cornered bobcat.

Maybe the wait was finally over. And pigs could fly.

A horse snorted, bringing Jace back from his reverie.

Sitting beside Marla, he considered letting her be the one to decide the mules' fate, but her plan was too flawed. He simply couldn't do it.

"Excuse me," Marla said, fanning his eyes with her outstretched, gloved hand. "Are you with me, Jace? You look like you're a zillion miles away."

Caught off guard, he cleared his throat. "I was only thinking," he confessed, mindful of his words. "I know you care about what happens to the mules, as I do, but there's a lot to think about here."

"Why do you assume you're right and my ideas are all wet?" Marla asked, her tone barely containing her frustration.

"You must realize Patterson isn't about to ship those mules anywhere," Jace said. "The bureau has the authority to send out a shooting party if they want to. If that's the throw of the dice, it would be the end of it. Certainly not the one we'd choose."

Marla's eyes blazed. "Never!"

"Face facts. We don't have a whole lot of time here."

She didn't speak for a moment, her face grim. "It isn't fair."

"Heck, fair went out in the third grade, or haven't you heard?" He paused. "Right now we ought to be thinking of ways to save the mules, not how we'd like things to be."

Marla let the wisdom of Jace's words seep in. It caused her to see him in a different light. He'd always been a giving man, ready to help his neighbors through tough times, not merely a rancher with a king-size ego, as she liked to think. She recalled having had a crush on him in her adolescent years, and a smile curved the corners of her lips.

"Maybe you're right," she said, the smile vanishing. "But just the same, I'm not quite ready to concede."

"Gaul-dang-it, Marla! You're one hardheaded filly."

Chapter Three

Marla watched Jace blow out his breath with resignation and get to his feet, offering her a hand up. "Let's move on," he said, his voice flat. She took his hand, feeling his warmth and strength through those curved fingers. He held her mare's head while she mounted, his eyes diverted.

Marla knew by the set of his mouth Jace harbored a bundle of resentment. Was she supposed to give in, just lay down and die, because he thought he was right? Actually, his ideas weren't over-the-top bad, but hers had validity too, even if he didn't want to recognize them.

Neither spoke as they rode on. Then Jace broke the ice. "By the way, how's your dad feeling? I want to get over to the hospital to see him this evening."

Marla liked the deep, resonant sound of his voice. "He's better. Thanks for asking." She stretched in the saddle. "Do you ride out here often? The view's wonderful, isn't it?"

He shrugged. "Haven't done it since the last roundup. Found an arrowhead in a cave up ahead." He reached in his pocket, pulled out a carved piece of stone, and handed it to her.

Marla examined the small object carefully, feeling its coolness in her palm. "Quite a find. Real Indian or made in Taiwan?" She grinned and handed it back, half expecting him to take offense at her stab at humor.

Jace grinned. "Got me there. Anyway, it's my good luck charm." He examined the arrowhead as if he hadn't taken notice of it in a long time. Then he ran his thumb over the dull edges before slipping the stone back in his jeans pocket.

Marla touched a round turquoise pendant resting at the base of her throat, a gift from her grandmother. They'd been the best of friends before she'd passed away. Thinking about the good times they'd shared, Marla felt a lump in her throat as she raised the turquoise to show Jace. "Speaking of good luck charms, Granny Martha gave this to me when I graduated from high school."

"I remember her. Nice lady. You take after her. She had a reputation for being quite a horsewoman and could ride like the wind."

"Yeah, that was Granny, all right." She dropped the turquoise back into place. "Funny how people like to keep good luck charms." She let a smile warm her face. "Maybe growing up just means we're still big kids deep down."

He chuckled. "I think you just may be right, bright-eyes."

A bird twittered and Marla followed its path from one bush to another as the small bird searched for insects.

"See its red head," she said. "I'd adore owning that one, but I wouldn't have the heart to cage it."

"Wild things should never be caged," Jace said, his eyes taking on a serious cast. "That goes for the mules, except there's no other way now."

"You sincerely believe that, don't you?" she said.

"Their survival's at stake. That's the long and short of it."

Jace scanned the valley, then swung his gaze back to Marla and studied her, making her heart flutter inside. His hazel eyes, with their flecks of green, turned guarded, as though he was keeping some inner thought to himself.

"How about lunch one of these days?" he asked, taking her by surprise.

Marla caught her breath. "If I can pick the place." Then she could have bitten her tongue. The glib words made her sound like a control freak. Could she quite possibly be one? Her relationships with men hadn't been exactly harmonious. Instinctively, she wanted to blame those she'd dated, but she wondered whether there might be something in her personality that needed a bit of tweaking.

"Fine with me," Jace said, breaking into her introspection. "But I'm afraid it's Molly's Coffee Shoppe or McDonald's."

She chuckled. "Molly's. She makes super salads. But I'm pretty tied up right now."

"When, then?" he persisted.

"How about Sunday?" she suggested, hoping he didn't catch on to the enthusiasm she was feeling.

"Sure."

She glanced up at the splendid way the midmorning light splashed against the mountain, ringing the valley with peach and gold tints like an artist's pallet. A deer scampered from a clump of brush, startling the horses before disappearing on small noiseless hoofs.

Marla's heart swelled. "I love the countryside. Why, I'd like to have a log cabin smack-dab in the middle of this valley. I'd sit on the porch and write poetry and day dream all the time."

Jace grinned. "Hey, now you're talking like a country girl. Where's the gal who was talking about moving to the city so she could teach?"

Her arms sagged. "We don't always get what we want."

The strange flicker in her eyes confused Jace as he looked at her. She had a girl-next-door smile and a killer body. He really didn't know the adult Marla all that well. What had she been doing during those years she'd been away besides taking college classes? Was she dating someone? Heck, she could even be engaged for all he knew. She certainly was too pretty not to have men flock to her. Strange, the mere thought made him jealous.

"Better be heading back," he said gruffly.

Marla scrutinized his face. "Yeah," she answered.

Farther on, they came to an outcropping. "Let's take a look on the other side," he said, his mood lightening. "Might catch a glimpse of those mules. One way or another, they have to be relocated pretty darn soon."

They drew the horses up. Marla let Jace help her dismount, his arm fastening around her waist. Before he set her on her feet, their eyes briefly locked. She found herself captured in his clear gaze and masculine embrace.

Though she'd never admit it, Marla felt a thrill course through her body. Then he let her go and she breathed easier.

Jace strode toward the base of the outcropping with Marla two steps behind him and turned, cocking his head to one side. "It'll take a little climbing. You up to it?"

She felt that tingle of exasperation that only Jace could induce. "What do you take me for—a sissy?"

He grinned. "Still got that tomboy tendency? Good. You'll need it."

She shook her head in mock dismay before she glanced up at the outcropping. Maybe she was biting off more than she could chew. It wouldn't be the first time. Reminding herself she wasn't a kid anymore, she said, "Lead on, McDuff."

He eyed her. "Hug the rock while you move upward and don't look down. It's only a little way." Then he added, "You first, as the gentleman said," making his voice sound gallant. "Don't worry, I'll catch you, if you take a tumble."

Marla took an additional glance. "Geez, I'm not so sure . . ."

Jace interrupted. "Is this the gal who said she could hold her own in any situation?"

"I said that a long time ago."

"Now don't play chicken. You'll be sorry if the mules are on the other side and you miss a chance to locate them."

Marla didn't wait for him to dare her. Reaching out for a handhold, she tried to stretch her jeans-clad leg up to the first boulder, without success.

Jace planted his brawny hands on her hips and gave

her a boost. Out of the corner of her eye she caught the unreadable light that flashed over his features.

"Just be careful," he said. "Don't want you getting your pretty knees messed up."

Taking a second, tentative step, Marla's heart clambered in her throat, whether from the risky climb or Jace's unexpected boost, she didn't know. Having committed herself, she slowly advanced up the side of the cold, hard rock, realizing she was out of condition. "This is no piece of cake," she gasped. Darn it, why had she agreed to take this little climb in the first place, and just what was she trying to prove?

Several feet below her, Jace called encouragingly, "Keep on moving. You're doing fine."

"Oh, tell me about it!" she said in a shaky voice, half expecting disaster to arrive any second. Her boot dislodged a small rock, which fortunately missed Jace's head before pinging off a boulder below.

A few more steps and her hands curled around the lip of the outcropping.

"Hold on a minute," Jace said. He climbed around her and hefted his body over the side until he was kneeling above her. "Now give me your hands."

Marla glanced up at him and his strong, outstretched hands. If she let go of her tentative hold and he missed grabbing her, she would be riding thin air for an eternity of moments before hitting a rocky bottom. The thought of making a wrong move caused her stomach to churn.

"Come on," Jace said, his gaze fixed on her.

Marla took a deep breath and let him grasp her wrists. He lifted her into his arms with seemingly little effort as he braced and stood up. She clung to him fiercely until she realized she was out of harm's way.

"Nice," he said as she began to pull away, a sensuous grin on his face.

"You might not consider this climb much of a challenge, but I do," she said in a tart voice, ignoring his look, which actually caused a tremor to arc down her spine.

Jace laughed softly. Still a trifle shaky from the climb, Marla sat on the smooth stone floor and breathed in the clean air, holding it in her lungs for a long moment. Jace didn't appear any worse for wear, though she was sure her own face was flushed with exertion and sweat.

"Look at that view," he said. "The buttes and mesas seem close enough to touch. Those two on the left remind me of some I saw in Chaco Canyon, the ancient Anasazi Indian preserve. The sun slices right through them like a dagger."

Marla turned an incredulous eye to him. "I'd like to go there sometime."

"I'll take you."

She smiled. "This is breathtaking, Jace. All of it. And if I'm not wrong, that row of trees over to the left is my ranch. What do you think?"

He strained to get a better look in the direction she indicated. "Yeah," he said. "Darn if it isn't."

She felt exhilarated. "I think I climbed up here once when I was little girl. It was during my exploring stage."

"Oh, yeah?" he asked with a grin.

Marla nodded, shielded her eyes with her hand, and let her gaze pan across the spectacular canyon beyond.

"See any mules?" he asked.

"No such luck." Then something caught her attention. "Isn't that a wide swath of grass up in the foothills? It looks dark green."

"Probably nothing more than shadows playing tricks on you, hon," he said.

Marla sighed with disappointment, then thought about Jace's calling her hon. It sounded so natural, like she was a child again, but the look in his eyes definitely revealed he no longer saw her as a child. It was the expression of a man when he's looking at an attractive woman.

"There's a small spring-fed stream over there," Jace said, pointing, "if it isn't dried up. Maybe we can water the horses on our way back. Might even pick up the herd's tracks."

"I thought you were going to tell me the herd was grazing over there in lush, thigh-deep grass," she said, disappointed.

His brow rose. "Don't I wish."

"I hate to think the mules are suffering," she said, unable to keep the concern from her voice. "Yet I can't see the wisdom of making them work-horses, either. Heaven only knows where they came from and what kind of lives they led."

Jace picked up a pebble and skimmed it across the rocks. "I doubt many of them will be used as work horses. Mules can be real devilish. I've had ol' Gen for years, and I can tell you some interesting stories."

"I know they're great pack animals. Tell me about her."

"Gen's played a lot of tricks on me. One day on a cattle drive she suddenly decided she didn't want to go any farther. Delayed the trip for over an hour when she laid down and wouldn't get up. I checked her out and there wasn't anything wrong with her. We had to remove the pack and repack the whole blessed load. Then she rose to her feet and shook herself like a dog. We put it back on and darn if she didn't sit down again. Finally, we had to remove half the load and redistribute it to the horses. She liked that, got up, and that was that."

"The pack was too heavy. She let you know the only way she could."

He laughed. "Oh, Gen's smart, all right. Another time we used her on a search-and-rescue mission when a light plane went down in a canyon not far from here. She seemed to understand perfectly the importance of it all and didn't try any shenanigans. We found the man half dead and brought him out on a litter pulled by Gen. She never hesitated or faltered once along some pretty treacherous cliffs. Got the guy down safe and sound."

"Did he live?" Marla inquired.

"Last I heard. Mules are plenty smart, contrary to what people say."

"Stubborn as a mule must mean smart as a whip," Marla said. They shared a chuckle. After enjoying the light moment, she grew serious, thinking about how a mule was the sterile offspring of a horse and a donkey. "The herd won't be reproducing itself, Jace. When they're gone, they'll be gone forever." She swallowed hard past the lump in her throat.

"I know," he agreed with a nod.

The sun glistened off the trickling stream in the distance as it moved sluggishly over a ribbon of small, gray stones. Marla turned back to Jace. "Thanks for bringing me here. It's really beautiful, even with the drought."

He gave her a quick grin, then said out of the blue, "You've grown into a real pretty woman, Marla."

His compliment made her heart skip a beat. Not knowing quite what to reply, she thanked him, then added, "We ought to be going now."

Needing to distance herself from his intense gaze and the personal compliments that played on her mind, she veered too close to the ledge. Jace reached out and took her hand firmly in his. His callused grip was reassuring. "Careful," he said. "It's a long drop. Here, let me help you down."

The alarm in his voice surprised Marla. Did he think she was going to take a swan dive over the side? "Okay," she said, and waited for him to make the next move.

He kept a firm grip on her arm as he took one last look around. "Awesome, isn't it?" he asked.

"Like being in an airplane, only better. Do you think it will stay this way? I don't want to see any developers invading it with cookie-cutter houses. Nor any freeways slicing through it, either."

A tiny tick quivered at the corner of Jace's eye. "You're passionate about a lot of things, aren't you?"

She hadn't thought about it. "Maybe."

Smile lines formed around his mouth, warm and genuine. "Ready to leave all this behind?" he asked.

"For now," she said, realizing that on the descent he'd be touching her again, and not quite sure it was a good thing.

Chapter Four

J ace took the lead, and with scarcely a pause, plunged over the granite lip. Marla glanced down only to experience an unexpected vertigo and shrank back, muttering, "Oh, wow."

Jace called to her. "Come on. You can do it."

Marla swallowed hard, refusing to let fear make her look foolish in Jace's eyes. However, dangling her legs over the side was the last thing she wanted to do. She took a couple of deep breaths but they didn't help that much.

"Got a problem up there?" he asked.

"No," Marla replied in a sharper tone than she meant to. "Why should going down be any harder than climbing up?" But it was. *Okay, girl, get a grip,* she told herself. Grasping her lower lip between her teeth, she swung cautiously over the side. Then her foot slipped on a rock, giving her a fright. She glanced down and saw

Jace reach for her, and let her body slide the remainder of the way into his comforting arms.

The power of his protecting grasp made Marla feel secure. "Thanks," she said, and stayed there a moment until he set her on her feet. Their cheeks lightly grazed, the rough texture of his day old whiskers teasing her senses. She thought for an instant he would kiss her— even wanted it to happen, but he let her go instead.

They were almost down when Marla said, "Oh, look," and pointed to an outcropping over to their left. "Is that a small dog up there on that ledge?"

Jace stopped in his tracks and studied the animal perched on the edge. "Would you believe it's a young mountain lion?"

"No!"

"I think so, and it appears to be stuck up there."

"Oh, dear. We have to do something," she said, thinking this was not a good thing. "We can't go off and leave it. Gosh, I wonder how in the world it got there."

"Must have slipped."

The small mountain lion made an attempt to get off the ledge and almost fell. It shrank back and hissed. Marla thrust out her hand in a reflexive motion. "What'll we do, Jace?" she cried.

"You got any ideas?"

She shook her head.

"I don't see how we can even get over there."

She gave him a hopeful look. "We could call in a rescue unit."

"They wouldn't come out for a wildcat."

"C'mon," she said. "We've got to do something."

Grumbling, Jace began to climb up the rocks at an angle and Marla followed, hoping they didn't come across a rattler. Then, taking another precarious turn, they found themselves just above the mountain lion.

Jace leaned over and took a look. "It's not much bigger than your old tomcat," he said.

He got down on his hands and knees and leaned over the side.

"Be careful," she cautioned.

"I'm going to try to sort of rappel within reach of the little critter and scoop him up, if I can," he said.

Marla held her breath as Jace let his body dangle over the rock formation. He swept his long arm down and grabbed the mountain lion. Pulling back from the ledge with his free hand, he almost slipped. Marla's stomach turned upside-down and she seized his ankle.

"I'm okay," Jace said.

He got a foothold and was safely on his feet again, cuddling the animal to his chest. Once the shock wore off, the young mountain lion resisted with sudden gusto. Jace let the fiesty animal go. It dashed away without even a thanks, having scratched the top of Jace's hand.

"You're hurt," Marla said as she examined it.

"It's nothing," he said, drawing his hand away from her. "I'm lucky the little guy didn't take a bite out of me. They can be pretty fierce."

"Nevertheless, you need to have it cleaned. I've got a bottle of antiseptic in my saddlebags."

They finished the short descent. Marla retrieved a small bottle and poured some of the solution over his hands.

"Ow!" he cried.

Marla grinned. "Big baby."

"That's a treatment no man likes. Well, thanks anyway."

Jace strode to his horse and tightened the saddle cinch he'd loosened earlier. His encounter with the mountain lion had somehow endeared him to her, even though she was trying hard to be indifferent. Why was she having these mixed emotions where he was concerned? And why had those memories of him flitted in and out of her mind when she was trying to sleep last night? He'd never meant anything to her. Well, maybe that wasn't quite true.

Jace tightened her mare's cinch too, then turned soft eyes on Marla and cupped his hands together to give her a lift up. "Ready for a boost?" he asked.

Marla started to say she didn't need any help getting on her horse but changed her mind. "Yeah, I could use a boost," she said. Carefully placing her boot in his hands, she sprang onto the horse's broad back. Jace handed her the reins. "There you go, now." Their fingers touched briefly, the sensation exciting her.

With an ease of motion, Jace gripped the pommel and mounted the big gray gelding. They rode on, letting the horses wander down the trail at their own pace. The temperature climbed. In no time his shirt clung to his body, revealing the splendid conformations of his chest and back muscles. Marla missed nothing.

Sparks of sunlight danced from the pale blue water as they approached the dwindling stream. The horses lowered their long necks and swallowed, making audible noises.

"I don't see any hoof tracks that might belong to the mules," Jace said after a quick look around.

Marla scrunched her mouth. "They couldn't have been here recently, but maybe they're farther up in the hill country eating salad greens. You're giving in too easily. As for me, I think I'll go on. I can't believe all the grass has dried up."

"Believe it. My cowhands and I explored nearly every inch of the valley. It was grim going." He lowered himself to the soft ground beside the stream and dipped his hat on his forehead as though he intended to take a nap. "It's peaceful out here."

Suddenly Marla wasn't in any hurry to keep up the fruitless search, and she sat beside him. "This place has a mesmerizing view of the valley, doesn't it?"

"It's mostly ours," he said.

She tossed him a surprised look. "I didn't know you owned land this far away."

"We left a few head of cattle here but brought most of them in closer. Looks like this stream will probably dry up in a few days. I'll send some of the boys to bring in the rest of the herd."

"It'll be hard on the wild animals as well." Marla pulled her own hat brim lower to shade her face and leaned back on her elbows. Things had gotten more complicated than she realized.

Jace sat up and reached out to remove her hat, then gazed deeply into her eyes. In the next moment he bent and brushed her lips with his, causing time to freeze as a reaction to the small intimacy.

"Sweet," he murmured. "Just like I knew they'd be."

Astonished, Marla gasped. She wasn't sure whether

she should wallop the man or wrap her arms around his neck and beg for more. However, he didn't try to embrace her, merely laid on his back and covered his face with his hat.

Marla found her voice. "What was that all about?"

"Whatever you want to make it," he said.

"That's easy, then," she sputtered, setting her hat back on her head, "because I want to forget it ever happened."

"Then I apologize." He sounded anything but apologetic.

Marla scrambled to her feet. "I don't have time to sit here and play boy–meets–girl games," she sneered.

Jace put down a hand and lumbered to his feet. "Then you don't choose to forget it happened?"

"I didn't say that."

He failed to hide his amusement. "Okay, sunshine. Have it your way."

They scarcely spoke on the return ride. Marla had a lot of thinking to sift through, and Jace Van Garrett was the subject she kept coming back to. His feathery kiss kept imposing itself upon her, making her lips tingle pleasantly. Yet with all her problems, she knew this was no time to be thinking of romance.

They crossed over onto Shelton land. Marla turned in the saddle and faced Jace. "There's a lot riding on the question of the mules," she said. "I don't trust Patterson's judgment. Those mules can mean nothing to a bureaucrat. He might even tell the ranchers to hunt them down and shoot them at will."

Jace flinched. "Don't you think I'm aware of that?"

Marla fought to keep her self-control. "Of course I

do." When he didn't reply, she said a might too sharp, "You're so . . . one way. Your way."

He shook his head. "What brought that on? And it's not true."

Feeling contrite, she let her shoulders droop. "I'm sorry if I sounded short tempered, but . . ."

Jace gave her a long, appraising look when she paused. "No harm done," he said. "But you realize we still have to come to an agreement and it might as well be right here and now."

Marla sighed heavily. "I've gone over it in my mind a number of times." Hadn't Patterson already indicated he wouldn't side with her? Then, too, maybe she just hated surrendering power. Considering this, she said grudgingly, "Oh, all right. We'll go with your suggestion."

He dropped the reins on the horse's neck and folded his arms over his chest. "I don't hear agreement here. I hear frustration and anger."

Marla wasn't a good loser. "Well, what do you expect?"

"We could flip a coin," Jace said, not cracking a smile. Moisture sheened his forehead. The weather had grown hotter, the sun baking the land even drier.

Jace looked so deadly serious, Marla had to smile. "Has it come to that?"

Marla had conceded and Jace was glad, convinced his was the better strategy for saving the mules. However, he knew it had caused hard feelings. He'd called her to confirm their going to lunch on Sunday but she'd told him it would have to wait until another time. What had he expected?

Jace's next best idea was to drive over to the Shelton ranch and see if there was anything he could do to help before the mule roundup got underway. With any luck, the roundup would take less than a week. He pulled his truck up beside the barn and put the gear in park. An old tomcat wandered away from the barn door.

Jace killed the engine. Marla seemed unaffected and definitely her own person. He smiled to himself, liking her spirit, as well as that softness she tried to hide. Her body was trim, her clear eyes vibrant, nose narrow, figure . . . well, he shouldn't be thinking about that.

Marla heard the truck pull up and glanced down through the upstairs bedroom window. She'd brought a load of fresh-smelling laundry and put it on the bed to fold. Her mother was in town visiting her father at the hospital and Marla was quite alone.

"What could Jace possibly want now?" She rubbed her nose. "And here I am looking like a total mess, besides."

Jace unfolded his long legs, stretched to his full height, and sauntered across the yard to the gate that kept the farm animals out of her mother's garden.

Marla secretly harbored a barrel full of resentment, even though she'd let Jace make the final decision about the mules. She slowly descended the stairs, knowing he was waiting at the door.

Jace stood framed by the screen door. He looked handsome in his tight jeans and navy blue shirt with the pearl buttons. The shirt showed off his wide shoulders and broad chest that tapered to a slim waist. Definitely not his usual work clothes. Had he dressed up a little to impress her or was he on the way into town to impress someone else? Everyone knew he could have his share of female company anytime he chose.

"Hey," she said, letting him stand on the other side of the threshold.

His neatly combed hair was damp from having showered, and his cheeks and chin freshly shaved, he said in a casual voice, "Came by to see if you need anything." A slight indentation marked where his hat had rested.

Marla resisted the impulse to smooth his forehead. "Hmm, I can't think of a single thing, but thanks all the same." She peeked over her shoulder. "I'm expecting a call or I'd invite you in," she said, the little white lie suspended between them.

Jace wasn't a man easily deterred. His gaze roved over her and his eyes fastened on her bare legs, a grin wrapping around his mouth. "Nice shorts. Cut just right."

Embarrassed, Marla said, "I do wear other clothes besides jeans, you know. Besides, it's hot."

He shoved his free hand in his pocket. "Can't wait to see you in a dress."

She threw him a disdainful look. "Yeah. Well."

"Going to the barn dance after the rodeo?"

"I doubt it."

He took a different tack. "Say, what's the real reason you're not inviting me in? I've been taught not to bite."

Marla thought about it and reluctantly stood back, opening the screen to let him pass through. He ambled into the living room, his boots thudding on the hardwood floor. She let the door slam shut and followed him. He politely stood there a moment grasping his hat until she waved her hand toward her father's leather chair by the unlit fireplace. Then he lowered his body into it, extended his legs and crossed his ankles in front of him.

"How's Charlie?" he asked, breaking the impasse she'd created. If he noticed a definite chill in the air he didn't respond to it. "I saw him at the hospital last night. Don't think he makes a very good patient. He was thumping that call button like it was a video game, exasperating the nurses no end."

Marla chuckled. "I think Dad's getting a little better every day. He told us he was like John Wayne in *Rooster Cogburn,* who said, 'My tail feathers may droop a little, but I can still out crow anything in the barnyard.' "

Jace enjoyed a laugh. "That sounds like Charlie. He never was one to give in easily."

"Dad's tough, all right, and he'll mend in time but it's going to be rough going for a while." She reached back and French braided her hair off her face. It was cooler that way.

The conversation waned. She wasn't sure whether she wanted him to go or stay, especially since she looked a sight. Then he got to the real reason he'd come. "I called Patterson and told him what we'd agreed on. He seemed relieved and wanted to know when we could start rounding up the herd. I said tomorrow morning, if that's okay with you."

"Tomorrow!"

"We're short on time." He paused. "By the way, I can lend you a couple of my guys to help out."

Marla considered this. "If you have extra hands, why don't you take them on the roundup? You don't need me."

Jace hesitated. "I don't think that's a good idea. You ought to be there, since Patterson talked to us both. The job won't be over until we bring 'em in."

Privately, Marla would have hated to miss going along but she didn't want Jace to know it, since it was in her nature to like her little secrets. She let his words hang briefly. "I'm awfully busy, what with Dad being gone."

"That's why I'm offering my hired hands."

Marla relented. "All right. What time are you leaving?"

"First light."

"But I've got a ton of things to do first."

He shrugged. "Just bring you and your mare. I'll have everything else ready to go."

"Ol' Gen going along?"

"Wouldn't dream of leaving her behind."

He rose. She realized she hadn't offered him coffee or an iced tea, not even a glass of water, but it was too late now. "See you tomorrow then." On a whim, she asked, "Got a date tonight?"

"Maybe."

"Oh."

Jace took a long step to where Marla stood, reached out to take a strand of her hair that had escaped the braid, and examine its texture between his fingers. His concentration made her feel uncomfortable and she pushed his hand away. He let her hair fall back into place.

"If you don't mind, I've got plenty to do," she reminded him.

Jace threw her a half smile. "Sorry."

He followed her to the door and said good-bye. She purposely flipped the lock behind him. So Jace was finally seeing her as the woman she'd become and not a kid in pigtails. Fine, but he could keep his hands to himself. She wasn't a Persian carpet to be closely examined. From the window, she watched him put the pickup in gear and turn around. A hen skirted across the barnyard in front of him, flapping its wings and clucking an insult.

The sun drifted behind the mountain range outside Molly's Coffee Shoppe. Marla sat across the table from her friend, Judy Longdon, enjoying the Monday night spaghetti dinner special. The town of Coyote Springs had only about three hundred inhabitants and the coffee shop was a popular eatery.

"Tomorrow we're leaving on the roundup," Marla told her childhood friend. She'd explained everything to Judy, even her ambivalence concerning Jace Van Garrett. "I can't wait for it to be over. He got his way where the mules are concerned. That's all he wants." She didn't care if she sounded petty.

"I hope you'll be back in time for the rodeo and barn dance. It ought to liven things up around here. Everyone's so depressed over the drought. As for your nemesis, there'll probably be a dozen gals vying for Jace to dance with them. I for one wouldn't mind spending a few minutes in his arms. Beats shucking corn."

Marla dismissed the idea. "We'll be back. You can count on it. Jace said something about entering the rodeo bull riding competition. Probably wants to impress the townfolk, I'm thinking."

Judy giggled. "It's a guy thing."

Judy didn't take life too seriously and could see the humor in most anything. Though the two women were opposites, their personalities complimented one another. Even their coloring and hair were different, Judy being of Native American heritage with dark brown hair and eyes the color of coal. Marla's skin was a light olive and her hair a dark blond with a hint of red.

"Since you got back, you've spent too much time on the ranch," Judy said, breaking into Marla's thoughts. "Why not take a fun break when you can?"

"You don't understand, I'm busy with a capital B," she said with a grin, then added in a more serious tone, "Ranch life has its rewards but can be isolating, too."

"Well?"

"I'll probably go," she said. "But I have to get through the mule roundup first. Actually, I'm looking forward to it. Haven't been on one in years." She chuckled. "Hope I'm up to it."

"Your eyes glitter when you mention going."

"It's the Jace Van Garrett part I'm not looking forward to."

"Uh huh. Now tell me what you really think."

Marla scrunched up her nose. "He's nice looking. Good bod. But full of himself."

"Way cool, is what I call him. Now tell me what else is rattling around inside your head that you're keeping from me, girlfriend?"

"Roundups can be a challenge," Marla said. "Then there'll be . . . uh . . . you know—a big lack of privacy."

Judy giggled. "You'll manage. Maybe you'll even find out why he's so well liked by the gals. You've got to admit he's loaded up with charisma. Now don't turn your nose up."

"There you go again. You want to be a matchmaker.

Is that it? Well, having another relationship is the farthest thing from my mind, especially with Jace Van Garrett."

Judy rolled her eyes. "That last one was that bad, huh?"

"Don't ask."

Chapter Five

At dawn Jace found Marla in the stableyard saddling her mare. He'd brought along the two ranch hands he'd promised, and intoduced Mike Garvey and George Smythe to her. Mike was a square-built young man who looked like he could take care of himself, and George had some training working with cutting horses. This made Marla feel better. She was glad all the responsibility for the ranch wouldn't fall on Jeff Begay's shoulders, but wasted no time letting the men know he was in charge.

"The new trainer should be here by the time I get back home," she told them. "Thanks for filling in."

Marla, Jace, and the wranglers left on their quixotic quest. She was still a trifle resentful. One way or another, she'd keep up her end of the bargain.

Jace scanned a small map he held in his hands as his gray horse moved slowly forward. He glanced up when

Marla rode alongside. "Patterson hired a pilot to locate the herd," Jace told her. "That saves us a heap of time. The mules aren't far from where we were yesterday."

"I hope they haven't moved on somewhere else," she said. "That can happen."

"Yeah. It's called Murphy's Law."

Jace tucked the map in a saddlebag, leaned back in the saddle, and folded his hands behind his neck, his elbows jutting out at angles. He wasn't pushing the horses, since the temperature was bound to climb and drain them of energy.

"Darn drought. It's gone on for over a year and there's nothing saying it won't continue into winter," he said, lowering his arms.

"I'm not naive, Jace, I know that can happen," Marla replied.

She suspected he said that to bolster his conclusion regarding the mules. Well, he'd won, hadn't he? She looked around at the brittle land where an abundance of colorful wildflowers once grew.

Jace took up the reins, his eyes widening. "I never said you were naive, Marla."

"Sure," she huffed, unable to keep the frustration from her voice.

Jace switched to another subject. "I saw your new yearlings a while back. One in particular, a bay, took my eye. Looks like your dad bought some sound horseflesh at the last auction."

"I hope so," Marla said. She tried to bank the sudden irritation. "They should make excellent cutting horses, the best in the state."

The sun burned through the morning haze as the temperature escalated. They stopped at a watering hole to let the horses drink. The depth of the pond was pathetically low. Marla wiped her brow with a bandanna.

"This heat sucks every bit of moisture from the land," she said, imagining what damage it was doing to her face. "I hope we find the mules in time. Things couldn't look much grimmer."

"We'll find them," Jace said.

Marla didn't share his confidence.

The riders traveled most of the day before locating the mules in a draw. The lead mule caught the scent of man, raised its head and snorted. Jace directed the riders to back away so as not to spook the animal into making a run for it, the others flying after their leader. Too late. The deafening sounds of hoofs rattled the countryside as the herd made for open country. Jace swore under his breath as they took off after them.

Shadows lengthened before they were able to draw near the herd again. This time they stayed well back and let the mules get used to their scent. Marla named the lead mule, Topper, because he had an extra heavy forelock. The big mule paced around the perimeter of the others, keeping a lookout with its keen eyes for signs of danger. The animal bowed its neck then lifted its tail in an arc and hee-hawed. Marla chuckled at such antics.

"Let them see we mean no harm," Jace said in a low voice.

The riders dismounted near a sycamore grove and sat on the yellowing grass. It was too late to try to round the herd up and get them back to the loading corrals, which were near the train tracks in Coyote Springs.

"At least most of the ranchers I contacted will take a couple of the mules," Jace said. He'd already volunteered to take any left over.

"We intend to take two, as well," Marla said. "It would be heartless to separate them entirely."

Jace eased down beside Marla on the dead grass, picked up a wilted dandelion and rolled it in his palm. The petals fell apart and he tossed them aside, the breeze catching them. Marla cupped her knees under her folded arms and focused on the herd, trying to decide which ones to take home.

"It bothers me to see those mules grubbing the sparse grass rather than nourishing feed," Marla said as she watched them. "They're far too lean and some look sickly."

"Yeah," Jace said with a note of sadness in his voice.

The more Marla thought about it the more she came to realize Jace's suggestion to bring the mules in and farm them out was the right decision. Maybe she'd been away too long and had lost her feel for what was going on in the valley.

She glanced toward a jagged mountain range with a cloud-cover in the distance. "If only one of those clouds would get balloon-fat and swing our way," she said. "We could pop it with a peashooter and our worries would be over."

Jace let a grin spread across his features. "I'm afraid wishing won't make it happen, but go ahead and try."

"It'll be dark before long," she said.

He nodded. "I'll have one of the boys make a campfire." But instead of getting up, he reached out and stroked the back of her hand. "When was the last time I saw you?" he asked.

"Yesterday," she said, giving him a small smile.

He ignored that. "Let's see, it was at a roundup, maybe five or six years ago. You and that mare of yours were a terrific team. When we got ready to brand the steers, you tried to cut one of them away from the herd. The steer gave you a bad time but you did it."

"I remember," she said, and quietly withdrew her hand. "That steer was as ornery as a cornered bobcat. I was afraid he would gore the mare but she was on to him."

"Your mustang dashed back and forth in perfect precision with the steer until it finally gave up and let you guide it into the corral. You trained that horse mighty well."

Marla smiled at the recollection. "I enjoyed the whole thing."

Jaces's mouth twitched. "So you intend to be a school marm?" he asked, switching subjects.

"Yes. I want to teach very much."

"I could have sworn you said a few years back you wanted to be a vet."

She grinned. "I did until I saw blood. Changed my mind real fast."

He laughed, then put a hand down, scrambled to his feet, and reached for her hand. "We'll gather the herd in the morning. Don't want to scatter them in the dark." He turned to the wranglers. "Let's make camp nice and quiet-like, folks."

Marla wasn't sure waiting was a good idea. "Don't you think we ought to go in now. They could slip away in the wee hours, Jace. You know, get spooked by a mountain lion."

The corners of his mouth turned down and his thick brows furrowed. He didn't speak for a moment, then said, "Slow down, gal. Your motor's running faster than a locomotive. Let's get one thing straight right here and now. I'm the trail boss, and I don't want any cockamamie arguments."

Marla bristled, feeling heat course through her veins. She was about to argue with him when she remembered the code of the trail. There could be only one leader. She reluctantly simmered down. The hired hands who witnessed the exchange looked every which way but at her and scurried to find kindling wood to make a fire. Swallowing her pride, she muttered, "Sorry, Jace."

He switched gears. "You mentioned hiring someone to help train the cutting horses while Charlie's laid up. Anyone I know?"

"I don't think so."

"What's his name? Good qualifications, I hope."

"Of course. He has excellent references." She didn't offer the man's name.

Jace took that in. "What did you say he's called?"

She pursed her mouth. "Grant Hull. He's from Florida."

"You checked him out with the Breeders Association?"

She smarted at the way Jace grilled her, as though she were some inexperienced teenager. "I'm not worried about a thing. Hull sent me Xerox copies of his credentials."

Jace gave her a quizzical look. "Didn't know they had

cutting horses in Florida. I thought it was only 'gator country."

"I'm sure he's the right sort of man who's kind to his mother, never runs a horse to death, and is always up at dawn. Seriously Jace, I know what I'm doing."

Jace shrugged and didn't ask another question. The wranglers pitched in and made camp. Soon smoke curled from the campfire. Jace dropped down beside Marla. On the trail he hadn't paid much attention to her, had even tried to keep his distance so he could concentrate. He took off his hat, sat cross-legged and chomped on a straw. The breeze whispered through the sycamores as the cowhand in charge of grub opened cans of chili and poured them into a big black pot. Marla looked tired and dust covered her face.

"Rounding up the mules will be anything but easy," he said. "We'll need to get a drop on them. They'll challenge us like we've never been challenged before."

"Why would they be any different from a herd of horses, or cattle for that matter?" she asked.

"I think they're smarter."

She shrugged. "I doubt you could convince horsemen of that."

"Wait and see. I think you'll change your mind quick enough."

She gave him a self-assured look. "I doubt it."

Chapter Six

The sun spread it's first pale fingers over the valley. Jace woke everyone. The riders rolled out of their bed-rolls, ate a cold breakfast of biscuits and honey washed down with strong boiled cowboy coffee, and packed up.

Marla prepared herself for the onslaught, every bone in her body aching from the night she'd spent on the hard-packed ground. Her hair was full of dust and she needed a shower, but water wasn't to be used for such luxuries. At least she'd brought along a change of clothes.

"I don't want any broken bones," Jace told his riders. "So watch it, okay? And I don't want the mules hurt. We'll go in clean-like and round them up." He glanced doubtfully at Marla, who'd just finished saddling her horse. "Everybody ready?"

"Gotcha." she said as she turned to mount.

They rode on slowly, picking up the pace when they got closer to the herd. The mules snorted, kicked up a ruckus, then thundered away, creating a dust storm. The wranglers took out after them. It was like the running of the bulls in Pamplona. The riders charged down a narrow draw and chased the mules into an opening surrounded by boulders. Jerome, one of the younger wranglers, leaped from his horse and made the mistake of grabbing one of the mules by the tail. The animal took off, racing in a wide circle. The cowboy sailed through the air like an unfurled flag, until he finally let go and skidded to the ground with a groan. He got up cursing, dusted himself off, and limped back to get the hat he'd lost in the free-for-all.

"Durn jenny!" he scowled. The mule brayed back at him. Everyone laughed.

With a raised hand, Jace gave the signal to continue before the cunning mules escaped.

"Ya! Ya! Ya!" the riders shouted in hard-charging pursuit.

The mules grunted and he-hawed, hardly knowing what hit them. Fortunately, when the dust settled, no one was worse for wear. Jace surveyed the herd. A dozen weary mules, their coats course and dull, stood quivering.

"We'll start back," Jace called to the riders. "Keep alert. These mules are as wily as coyotes."

They rode all morning without finding any grasslands. Near a grove of oak trees Jace ordered them to create a makeshift corral for the mules. Everyone needed a rest. Not fussy, the mules nibbled patches of weeds.

Todd, one of the men, laid out packaged lunches. "Peanut butter sandwiches and oatmeal cookies. Nothing fancy," he said.

Marla took a bite of her sandwich. "Tastes good." But it made her thirsty and the water supply in her canteen was low.

Jace gave a slight nod. They hadn't spoken for hours. A bee landed in her hair. "Oh!" she said, and batted at it.

"Hold still," Jace said. "Bumble bee on the loose." He reached out with his thumb and index finger and carefully removed the tiny insect before Marla could get stung, setting it on a bush. "There! Now fly away."

She marveled that he hadn't gotten stung. "Thanks," she said.

Amused, Jace said, "I'm trying to remember a nursery rhyme about a bee."

"You remember nursery rhymes?" she said, incredulous.

Jace was a man's man, over six feet tall with dark thick eyebrows and intense eyes. She didn't figure him for children's stories.

"I have a little nephew," he said. "The kid likes me to read to him."

"That's right. Your sister's boy. How is Debra?"

"Doing fine. Another baby's on the way. You ought to stop by and see her."

"I'd like to," Marla said. "We had a good time together when we were children."

"You were chatterboxes." He grinned and got to his feet. "Let's take a walk. It's a long ride back. Might as well stretch our legs." He reached down and helped her rise. Her braided hair curled at her throat. "That's pretty," he said in almost a whisper, "the way your hair curls."

Jace was so close his warm breath tickled her skin, causing her to shiver inside. She stepped back and pushed the hair away. "I think I'll pass."

Jace frowned and sauntered on. Five minutes later he was back.

"Let's mount, folks," he said.

Marla headed to where her horse was tethered to a bush, tripped on a tree root, and landed awkwardly on her hands and knees. "Darn it!" she groaned as stabs of pain gripped her kneecaps. Jace came on the run. Instead of laughing at her clumsiness as she half expected, his face became white.

"You all right?" he asked, and knelt beside her.

Marla found herself staring into his hazel eyes and temporarily forgot the pain. The closeness of his body caused her to feel giddy and a sudden heat flashed upward from her neck to her face.

For a moment she wanted him to take her in his arms and comfort her. His lips were tantalizingly close. Then she said, making light of her fall, "Nothing's broken, I don't suppose. Only my pride."

He looked uncertain. "You're sure now?"

Marla nodded and tried to rise but ended by wincing. Jace stood upright, concern mapping his features. "Here, let me help. Can you stand?"

Jace grasped her forearms and carefully helped her to her feet. Her knees stung with the action. "I didn't see it," she said as a way of explanation. "Foolish of me, tripping over a blamed root."

"Don't put yourself down, Marla," he said. "You must have caught the toe of your boot. Can you walk okay?"

"I think so." She grimaced when she tried but she steeled herself.

"I'm afraid you're going to have sore knees for a few days. You need to get home as soon as possible and put ice packs on them. I can send Jerome with you."

"Thanks all the same, but I'll be okay," Marla assured him.

He looked doubtful. She cringed at the thought of having to ride but wasn't about to miss any of it. And she wasn't a quitter.

Jace gently lifted her onto the horse's saddle as though she weighed no more than a child. "It's your call, hon."

Marla took the reins, feeling a trifle teary at his kindness. "I'll be fine," she said. "I won't hold you back."

He looked hurt. "I wasn't thinking of that."

Marla fumbled for words and forced a smile. "We better get moving." Then she realized she hadn't thanked him. "Thanks, Jace."

He tipped his hat and turned away. Marla's knees smarted under the fabric of the jeans. Finally, she pulled her legs out of the stirrups and let them dangle.

Jace broke into an old Western song, but quit when he couldn't remember the rest of the words. Marla chuckled in spite of her discomfort. Right on cue, a wild songbird flitted from bush to bush, warbling sweet chirps and trills that helped to get her mind off her injuries.

"Wish I could whistle like that," Jace said with a wink as the horses trudged along.

Marla nodded, thinking his voice sounded nice.

Toward sundown, the group rode onto Shelton land. "I'm too bushed to even yawn," Marla said.

Jace had somehow banked his fatigue, or at least it didn't show. He turned to the wranglers. "Take the mules to my ranch and feed and water them. I'll be along directly." He pointed to the two mules Marla had indicated she wanted. "Leave those here."

They tipped their broad-brimmed hats to Marla and followed Jace's directions before pushing the herd on.

"You know you can always call on me any time if you need help," Jace told Marla.

"Thanks," she said. Her spine ached from being in the saddle so long, and her knees throbbed.

Jace stayed with her as they headed over to the barn. Jeff Begay greeted them, then took charge of the mules. Jace insisted on carrying Marla into the house.

"Really, this isn't necessary," she said.

"Quiet, woman."

Jace placed her on the sofa in the living room and slipped a pillow under her head, then hurried to the kitchen to make ice packs. While he was away, she got up and hobbled to the laundry room to find the shorts she'd worn before she left. Dropping her jeans around her ankles, she stiffly kicked them away, wiggled into the shorts, and hobbled back to the sofa just as he emerged from the kitchen.

"So you're a quick-change artist?" he asked, amusement dancing in his eyes. However, one look at her knees and he sobered. "The skin isn't too scratched but your knees are swollen and I'll bet they hurt like blazes. Why didn't you tell me?"

"Actually, I feel better now," she said.

Jace didn't look convinced. He stood over Marla like one of the ER doctors on television. All he needed was a mask and a scalpel. She almost laughed but thought better of it. He was trying to be helpful, wasn't he?

"Here we go," he said, and carefully positioned the ice packs he'd made from plastic freezer bags and tea towels.

She shuddered. He sat on the floor and examined his handiwork. His gaze wandered down the length of her legs and he swallowed hard before breaking his stare. "Nice," he said.

She knew he was referring to her bare legs. One part of her felt embarrassed but another part was glad he admired them. After awhile, he got up. "Your mom's not here?"

"She spends a lot of time at the hospital."

"I'll fix you something to eat," Jace said.

She straightened. "You don't need to do that."

He caressed her face with a smile. "I insist, sunshine. Can't have you starving. I'll poke around in the fridge and see what I can find."

She watched him saunter away, the outline of strong back muscles projecting against his shirt.

Jace left after Marla had eaten a bowl of minestrone soup and soda crackers. And he called twice the next day to check on her. On the third, when she assured him the pain was gone, he brought over a three-month-old puppy, the spitting imagine of Buck, the dog they'd had to put down due to a fatal illness.

Jace thrust the furry puppy into her arms as she sat in a wicker chair on the wrap-around porch. "He's yours, hon. You'll just love the little guy."

Marla was overcome. "Well, how . . . ? My gosh! He's Buck all over again."

"Dad had our female, Suzy, bred to Buck. But you couldn't have known that since you were away at the time."

"I don't know what to say." Thrilled, she leaned forward and kissed Jace's cheek when he bent down. "Thanks so much. I'm speechless." She hadn't been so happy in ages.

Jace's face beamed. "Glad you like the little guy."

"What should I call him?" she asked.

"He answers to Little Buck but you can name him yourself, if you prefer."

"No way. This little fella's going to be Buck the Second—and that's that."

She cuddled the friendly puppy to her. He licked her face and wagged his tail, his belly round and cuddly. "It's love at first sight," she said with a warm smile.

Jace grinned. "And Little Buck's housebroken."

She sighed with relief. "That'll make Mom real happy."

Jace stuck around for a while then left, leaving Marla with a handful of wiggling joy.

Grant Hull arrived. He didn't look like what Marla had pictured—sort of scruffy, his eyes set too close together and his belly hanging over his belt. He was forty-four, of average height and a tad rotund, with big teeth and pink gums. Knowing the man was finally here to fill in cheered her.

"We're so glad to have you here," Marla said, then shook his hand. "I understand you worked at a well-known breeder's ranch. We really feel fortunate you decided to make the change at the last minute."

Hull's eyebrows connected in a unibrow. "I worked for a real nice horse farm in Florida," he said, then recited a litany of his accomplishments. "I left because I wanted to be nearer my family in Prescott. Mom's not getting any younger and has some health problems."

"I understand," she said, noticing his limp for the first time when he took a few steps. "Let me show you around."

He caught her looking at him. "Got thrown from a stallion when I was twelve," he said. "Won't interfere with my work none."

"No problem," she replied.

Marla was too relieved to have him on the ranch to bother about things like that. Her father was due to be released from the hospital in a matter of days but the orthopedist said he wouldn't be able to work for six months. She'd need to figure ways to handle him, knowing he'd want to get back to work.

They walked to the stables and Marla turned to Hull. "You got my letter about Dad?" Hull nodded. "He's a man who knows his own mind and will hate being confined. Hopefully, your being here will make him see he doesn't have to jump right back in."

Hull laughed, a strange sound that gathered in his throat like a horse's nicker but never got completely beyond. "I know that feeling, all right," he said. "Been laid up myself a few times."

Marla showed him the new horses. "You've got your work cut out for you," she said.

"Don't you worry about a thing, miss. I'll have them in shape in no time."

"Cutting horses are a wonder, the way they counter a cow when it wants to go back to the herd."

"Yeah, just show the horse what cow you want separated and he does the work pretty much by himself."

"That is, if the horse is well trained," Marla said. "That's what we do around here."

"Not a problem," Hull said with confidence.

Marla liked his attitude.

Jace came by the Shelton ranch and Marla introduced him to Grant Hull.

"Marla tells me you worked in Florida," Jace said, eyeing the man as though he was a foul smelling beef on the hoof, which annoyed her.

Hull's voice changed slightly, becoming a touch wary. "That was last fall," he said.

Marla frowned, thinking this rather odd. In Hull's letter, he'd indicated he was just now leaving his last place of employment, but she preferred not to question him in front of Jace. It probably wasn't important, anyway.

Jace didn't stay around long. Marla finished showing Hull the ranch, then took him to the bunkhouse where he'd be sleeping. Jeff Begay usually went home after work each day and no other hired hands were on the ranch.

"You've got the whole place to yourself," Marla said. He seemed to like that. "I'll let you settle in now."

Hull looked around the old building. "Thanks, Ms. Shelton. I'll start fresh in the morning."

Marla smiled. "We're really glad to have you with us. If you need anything, I'll be up at the house."

Hull gave her a broad smile. "This place will do just fine."

Marla thought the bunkhouse was rather shabby and was glad he seemed to think it would be adequate. The hint of a doubt Jace had put in her head vanished.

Chapter Seven

Marla rose early the next morning, dressed in jeans and a red shirt, then fed Little Buck, who had taken to sleeping on a rug in her bedroom. Marla thought it best to keep an eye on the puppy, since he probably wasn't out of the chewing stage. Her mother, JoAnn, was cooking pancakes at the kitchen range.

"I'm going to pick up your father this morning," JoAnn said. She looked more rested. "It will be a relief to have him home."

"It definitely will. Let me help you with breakfast." Marla took dishes down from an oak cupboard and placed them on the table, along with plaid placemats.

"You can take some pancakes to Hull," JoAnn said. "I hope he works out. I know how anxious you are to go away and teach."

"Mom, I told you I won't leave until Dad's on his feet again."

Her mother sighed. "That may take months. Your father isn't any spring chicken, and there's that rib fracture too."

"Don't worry about that now," Marla assured her. "He'll be right as rain in no time."

Marla's mother smiled, then handed her a plate of pancakes. "Here, will you take these to Hull? And don't forget butter and syrup."

Marla took a tin platter from a shelf, put everything on it, and pushed the screen door open with her backside.

Grant Hull was coming out of the barn when she rounded a corner and nearly ran into him. He shielded his eyes from the sun's glare with his big hand. His wide mouth cracked into a grin, exposing a space between his front upper teeth.

"That for me?" he asked, giving the pancakes an appreciative glance.

Marla nodded. "You must be hungry."

"Could eat a buffalo, and I don't mean them skinny little buffalo wings you get in cafes."

"Shall I put this in the bunkhouse?"

"Naw, I'll take it. And thanks kindly, little lady."

She handed him the platter and was about to turn away, when he said, "Fed and watered the horses already. I'll groom them after I eat these."

"Good." The man was on top of things. What else could she ask for? "Then you can work on training the new cutting horse afterwards. By the way, the bay yearling is pretty spirited. We want to bring him around slowly."

Hull scratched his unshaven jaw. "Yeah. I'll bring him 'round. He'll do just fine."

Marla strode back to the house, confident Hull would work out well.

Chapter Eight

Jace saddled his gelding. He thought about the stranger the Sheltons had hired and didn't much care for the look in the new trainer's eyes, though he couldn't quite put his finger on it. The Sheltons deserved someone honest and forthright but that wasn't the impression he received. Yet, Marla wouldn't listen to any contradictory remarks about him. Still, Jace had his suspicions. Maybe he was just suspicious by nature but he'd keep alert for anything that didn't look right, all the same.

Jace thought about Marla, admired her spunk, her fortitude, and she was darn pretty, too. In truth, in this short period of time, he'd become swept away by her. She made him want to protect her, to be more of a man. She brought out his soft side, even made him think of settling down and raising a family.

Jace spent the day with his ranch hands distributing the mules to reluctant ranchers, then drove to the Shelton ranch. Marla was grooming her mare when he parked and got out of the truck. Bettina shied away from him. Having mustang blood, the mare could be skittish.

"Whoa!" Marla called, and hung on to the lead rope. Jace stepped in and helped her calm the horse.

"What's up?" he asked, standing back from the mare.

"Nothing much." Marla led Bettina to the stables and Jace followed. He watched the subtle way Marla's hips swung and it stirred his hormones. Then he stepped around her to open the stall gate. Marla broke open a fresh bale of hay and they scattered it around the horse. Bettina lowered her head and foraged, grunting a low approval.

"Your new man paying his way yet?" Jace asked. "Hull's his name, right?"

"He seems okay."

"Keep your eye on him. He looks like the kind that cleans out the household silver."

Marla chuckled, and they walked away from the stables. "What a thing to say. Besides, we don't have any silver, other than my Indian beads. Hull doesn't look the type to be wearing turquoise."

Jace failed to laugh. "Didn't like the look he gave you."

"What look?"

"I can't quite put my finger on it. He's too glib, maybe," Jace added.

"That's funny, Mom says he doesn't talk enough. You can't both be right." She tossed him a grin.

"Yeah, well . . ."

"If you read his resume, you wouldn't be such a doubter."

"Oh? Where is it?"

Her eyes snapped. "I won't show it to you because it's none of your business. If Dad thinks Hull's all right, then that's your answer."

Jace backed off. How could he argue with that? "See you around, bright eyes. And by the way, don't forget the barn dance. You're saving the last dance for me, remember?"

"I never said that. Why, you didn't even ask me."

He grinned, then got back in the truck. She threw him a wave as he drove back the way he'd come.

Marla's mother couldn't have been happier to have her husband home and cooked all his favorite foods. She hovered around him until he told her, "Stop fiddling, JoAnn. You're driving me up the wall."

Marla sat across from him in the living room of the Queen Anne-style house while they played a game of cards. "We're just so glad to have you back," she said, her smile deepening.

Her father looked haggard, even older, after his hospital stay. The wrinkles on his face and neck were more defined, his eyes less vibrant. It worried Marla.

"How's the trainer working out?" Charlie asked, shuffling the cards.

"You mean Mr. Ice?" JoAnn answered.

Charlie swung his full attention on her. "I don't understand."

"Deficient in social graces. Stone-faced most of the time. Oh, I guess he's all right," his wife said.

"I don't understand about this face business," Charlie said. "Is he supposed to win a popularity contest? As long as he gets the work done, that's all I care about. We didn't hire him to be Mr. Personality."

Seeing her father's agitation, Marla was sorry her mother had said anything, not wanting her father to get upset. She was seeing a side of him she'd never seen before. He seemed less sure of himself but at the same time more short-tempered.

"Well, spit it out, girl," Charlie said, shifting his attention back to her. "Is something bothering you? You're sitting there staring at me like I'm a statue."

Marla chose her words carefully. "Hull will do just fine. No need to worry about a thing, Dad."

Her father ran his hand along his jaw, giving what she said consideration. "Has Jace talked to him?"

"A couple of times," she said.

"What did he say?"

"In truth, he didn't sound too impressed."

"I see." Charlie paused before dealing the cards. "Keep an eye on Hull, hear? I've always trusted Jace's judgment."

"Of course," she said, so as not to antagonize him. But his words hurt—a lot. Wasn't her opinion worth something?

After the game ended, Marla rose from the chair. "I'm going to town to get your prescriptions filled. Be back after awhile." She leaned down and kissed the top of her father's head.

Driving down the ribbon of road into Coyote Springs gave Marla time to gather her thoughts. For a while her mind wandered from one thing to another like a prairie dog's trail. She remembered her senior year in college

and Matthew Underhill, the student she thought she'd
fallen in love with. Both Matthew and Jace were congenial men, but that was where the similarity ended.
Matthew was bookish and introverted. Jace was ener-
getic and fun-loving, someone not above plunging into
anything he considered a good cause.

Thinking of Mathew, however, brought on a touch of
heartache. They'd been inseparable for awhile, even
talked about marriage, then he'd broken her heart when
she learned he'd been intimate with her roommate. That
had ended things fast, and not too prettily, harsh words
having been spoken. Matthew had tried to persuade her
it was nothing—just one of those things that happens.
Well it hadn't been nothing to her.

Marla asked herself if Jace would try something like
that. Certainly women gathered 'round him like bees to
honey. She admired his wit, the way he worked so hard
and didn't bat an eye when called to take on extra re-
sponsibilities. They were different kinds of men, all
right.

Marla chided herself. She'd never even dated Jace,
and they certainly didn't have anything she could call a
relationship. Yet the fear of making another big mistake
colored her thinking, and she told herself to cool it.

Marla drove past a cornfield on the edge of town, its
stalks had turned yellow. Just ahead, the school building
looked equally forlorn. No children would be playing
games in the school yard come fall. It made her sad. She
moved on down the street and parked in front of the
pharmacy.

On this hot, summer day, a few people stood in a
cluster under the outdoor overhead fan by the entrance.

The talk in town was not about the drought or the mules, but about the school's closing for good.

Marla picked up her father's medicine, then left the pharmacy and walked across the street to the post office to buy stamps. Two women who'd been ahead of her in school were discussing the same topic—the school closure—and scarcely took time to greet her.

On her way back to the ranch, Marla stopped at the school and peered over the chain-link fence. Seeing the gate unlocked, she sauntered around the building to the playground. How she'd love to make it come alive with children again and hoped with all her heart the school board would hire another teacher so the children wouldn't have to be bussed.

A sudden footfall behind Marla startled her and she pivoted around but there was no one nearby. Had she imagined it? Maybe it was the ghost of all the children who'd played here since the turn of the century. Then she laughed at her own imaginings.

On the drive back home, Marla turned in at the Van Garrett ranch. Debra, Jace's sister, had called earlier and invited her over. Marla looked forward to the short visit. She parked in front of the rambling ranch-style house and slid off the seat.

A swarm of gnats appeared like tiny flies and pestered her eyes. She swatted at them with the back of her hand and hurried toward the house. Jace was on his hands and knees on the sparse lawn playing 'giddyap' with Debra's three-year old son, Adam.

Having outrun the gnats, Marla stopped briefly to watch them. The child was a sturdy little fellow with blond hair and blue eyes. He looked like his father's side of the family.

Jace set the boy aside and lumbered to his feet. A man with a big frame and ease of motion, Marla couldn't help admiring him. And now she'd seen his soft side where children were concerned. She wished they could get along better but they were both strong willed, neither wanting to give an inch. That didn't make for a healthy marriage. Her stomach did an unexpected lurch. Strange that she should even think of marriage. She pushed the notion away and asked the boy, "Does your horse whinny and buck, Adam?"

"He rolls over and plays dead when he gets tired," Adam said, his expression serious.

Marla had to laugh.

Jace switched subjects. "Sounds like you're having engine trouble," he said. He got up and dusted himself off. "Release the hood and I'll take a peek." He disappeared into the barn and came back with a screwdriver and a wrench. Marla walked back to the SUV and popped the hood. Mercifully, the knats had disappeared. Ducking his head under the hood, Jace tinkered for a few minutes then told her to switch on the ignition. She did. It didn't purr like her one-eyed cat.

"Carburetor problem," he said, and wiped his hands on his thighs. "Better take it to Phil's in town. Say, what brings you to our fortress?" he said with a grin. "Out castle hopping? Adam, here, thinks he's a knight and I'm his trusted steed."

"What's a steed?" Adam asked. "Is it a broom?"

"No, it's a horse," Jace said.

"Uh-huh," Marla said. "Just thought I'd drop by and say hello to Debra."

"Go on in. But Deb's running late. I'm baby-sitting Adam. She went to town to get a haircut. Stay awhile and visit with Mom. Deb won't want to miss you."

"Wish I could. I'm on my way home and I've got a ton of things to do. But I'll stay for a few minutes if your mom isn't too busy."

"She's never too busy for company. You know Mom." He turned back to Adam.

Marla opened the screen door and called, "Mary, it's me, Marla," and let herself in when she heard, "Come on in, girl."

After a friendly exchange, Marla said, "I told Debra I'd come by but I'm real early. Would you tell her I'm inviting her to supper tonight? She told me her husband is out of town. I want to hear about that new kitchen floor they had installed."

"She'd love to," Mary Van Garrett said. "Jace and I can take care of Adam. Give her a breather. He's quite a handful."

When Marla got back home, she called her friend Judy to invite her too, but Judy had a date.

Chapter Nine

Hat in hand, Jace Van Garrett came to dinner carrying a bunch of red roses. "Picked them up at the supermarket in town," he said.

His sudden arrival took Marla by complete surprise. "Where's Debra?"

"She had to drive home to the ranch at the last minute. Some minor emergency, like the bathroom being flooded. Anyway, she's waiting for the plumber."

"I don't call that a minor emergency."

"Neither did she."

He held out the flowers. She took the blooms to the kitchen and put them in a vase with water. This was not going to be the evening she expected. Her parents had eaten earlier and her mother was reading to her father in the bedroom.

Marla would have put on fresh lipstick and a touch of blush had she known Jace was inviting himself over. She led him into the living room and he took a seat in the leather chair by the fireplace. Glancing around, he said, "Nice of you to have me over."

Marla wasn't quite sure what to make of this switch, yet she could just hear Debra saying, "You go in my place. Marla's gone to all that trouble." Well, she'd make the most of it. "Sure," she said.

Jace stared up at the enlarged photograph of her father on a cutting horse that hung over the mantle and he tilted his head.

"That photo was taken years ago," Marla said. "I love it. Dad won a special award that year."

She suddenly felt a tangle of emotions and said a little prayer that her father would recover fully. Fate could play such dirty tricks.

Seeing the anxiety on her face, Jace was on his feet in an instant and his strong arms pulled her into a comforting embrace. "You're worried about Charlie, aren't you?" he asked, his voice filled with empathy.

"I can't help wondering if he'll ever be the same. The leg broke in two places." She straightened and he released her. "Let me get you a glass of iced tea," she said. "The weather's hot."

Marla brought him back a tall glass from the kitchen and managed to get her emotions under control. Jace was standing by the fireplace, a bent elbow resting on the mantle. Their hands touched when she gave him the cold glass.

"Just what I wanted," he said, taking a healthy swig.

All at once Marla felt nervous. Jace was no stranger, but she wasn't accustomed to seeing him alone in this social context. Was the axis in their relationship turning? A warmth surged through her body. She picked up a magazine from the coffee table and fanned herself, then remembered the pot roast. "The oven," she said, jumping to her feet.

"I'll help," Jace insisted, and followed her into the kitchen.

Marla bent to open the oven door. "Let me," he said, and grabbed pot holders from a hook on a cabinet next to the stove. Using care, he removed the ruby-colored glass pot, setting it on the range top. "Smells real good."

Marla had laid out blue placemats and flatware at the kitchen table. The plates were on the countertop. Jace turned on the faucet and filled water glasses as Marla lifted the steaming roast and vegetables to a platter. Jace insisted on carving the succulent meat. Marla filled the plates and put them on the table, along with a green salad and hot biscuits.

"I hope everything tastes like it's supposed to," she said. "Cooking isn't my specialty."

"It'll be great." His eyes lightened. "I see you have other talents than a way with horses."

Marla found herself grinning. "Mom's a better cook."

She motioned for Jace to sit at the table across from her, and her pulse quickened as she glanced up and caught his cool eyes on her. He took up his fork and ate like a man who enjoys his food. No picky eater, this one, she thought with relief.

"Mm, this is real delicious, Marla. Better than my mom's, though I'd never admit it in front of her."

Marla smiled. "Thanks." She glanced down at her plate, the compliment making her feel better.

When they finished, Marla cleared the plates and took a berry pie down from the old pie saver. The free-standing cupboard had belonged to her grandmother. She sliced two crumbly sections and put them on dessert plates, then added a large dollop of whipped cream.

He tasted it. "Good," he said with a grin and took another forkful.

Jace helped her with the dishes afterward, then they strolled outside where the air was at least ten degrees cooler. The full moon and sparkling stars made it almost as light as at twilight. They tried to name all the constellations but Marla gave up.

"Astronomy wasn't one of my better subjects," she said. "I hate to admit it but I almost flunked."

"Who cares about stars, anyway?" Jace chuckled. "They don't brand cattle, cook a great meal like you did tonight, or run after wayward mules."

Marla laughed. She couldn't deny her attraction to Jace. But she quickly reminded herself not to get too close to him. She didn't intend to be one of the batch of young women in the valley who got burned.

"It's late and I've got to get up early in the morning," she said, by way of bringing the evening to an end. "We'd better head back to the house."

Jace looked displeased but didn't try to talk her out of it. Then he asked, "Can I see you again soon?"

"That would only complicate things," she said too quickly.

"What do you mean, complicate things? I've known you all your life."

"I'll be leaving when Dad's better and..." She couldn't think of another excuse.

* * *

Marla worked with one of the more wily yearlings who wasn't sure whether it wanted to be a cutting horse or a bucking bronco. Her father gave her encouragement from the disadvantage of the sidelines until his patience ran short. "Bring my crutches, pronto," he demanded.

Jeff obliged. However, Charlie's attempts to walk with the crutches in the sandy loom worried Marla for fear he'd fall. "Dad, take it easy," she said.

He paid no attention and struggled a few feet. Finally, JoAnn came hurrying across the yard. Hands on hips, voice raised, she said, "Charles, I saw you through the window. You want to get inside that corral, don't you? Well, the doctor said no. Now I insist you go into the house and rest before you break something else."

His face turned crimson and Marla could practically read the frustration ping-ponging around in his brain. "Oh, all right," he muttered. "But I'm no dang invalid, hear?" He handed Jeff the crutches and planted his bottom in the wheelchair.

Marla sighed with relief as her mother wheeled him away. "Poor Dad," she said. "This has really got to be hard on him. He's always been so independent."

Jeff gave a nod. "I'll take the crutches up to the house and put them on the porch."

An hour later, Jace strolled into the stableyard. "Thought I'd drop by and see if I could lend a hand."

"I'm about ready to wrap it up for the day," Marla said, exasperated at the lack of progress she'd made with the horse. "This one's got too much spirit and won't let me on his back."

"That right?" Jace asked. "Never heard of a horse having too much spirit."

"Hull worked with him this morning but I don't think he made much progress, either." She lowered her eyes with defeat.

"Where is this 'top' trainer from the alligator state?" he asked with disdain, glancing about.

"He's working with one of the horses in the far corral."

Jace took the yearling's reins from Marla. "What do you call this gelding?"

"Major, because he thinks he's boss."

Jace threw back his head and laughed. "You and your names." He ran a hand along the horse's sleek neck. "Okay, Major, let's walk around the corral, get used to each other."

The horse eyed Jace with suspicion and made a skittish move. Jace calmed him with a gentle tone of voice. Then he turned back to Marla. "What's gotten into this horse?"

"I don't know."

"He's a fine yearling but jumpy as all get-out. He doesn't trust me. I saw him a couple of weeks ago and he didn't show any fear then."

Marla's face tightened. "What are you driving at?"

Jace had his suspicions, and they involved Hull, but he didn't answer her question. Instead, he patiently led the reluctant horse in a wide circle, then made each circle smaller until they came to a halt. Man and horse stood side by side as though it was a perfectly natural act, then Jace quietly waited for a reaction. The yearling raised his graceful head and gave a low nicker. Jace didn't move an eyebrow. The horse reached around and sniffed Jace's shirt. Jace gently patted the horse's neck. Shifting its body, the horse pushed Jace's straw hat. The hat tilted over one ear and fell onto the dry ground. The horse edged back as though ready to flee, but Jace didn't react and the animal settled.

Marla tipped back on her heels, fingers in the back pockets of her jeans. "He's beginning to trust you," she said, reluctantly admiring his skill.

Jace grinned, then reached down in slow motion, picked up his hat, and placed it back on his head. Major stood watching him. Taking care, Jace raised his hand and let the horse sniff it before patting the animal's flank. This time Major showed no fear, merely made a muffled sound.

Jace turned his full attention back to Marla. "There's nothing wrong with Major. He only needs to know no one's going to yank him around."

Marla bristled. "Why, we're never cruel to our horses."

Jace acknowledged this. "How about Hull?"

"There you go again," Marla snapped. "Hull is perfectly aware of our rules."

"Then you better remind him," Jace said evenly. "This horse tells me someone hasn't been so gentle with him."

"What are you saying?"

"Just what I said."

He handed the reins to Marla and sauntered back the way he'd come without saying good-bye.

The sun was in a splendid descent behind the mountain range when Marla walked over to the porch and took a seat in a wicker rocking chair. She loved this time of day. Sitting quietly here seemed like a fitting reward after a long day of work. She thought about Hull. The trainer seemed to be doing well enough, in spite of what Jace intimated.

She pushed the bundle of doubts from her mind and whistled for Little Buck. The puppy whizzed around the corner of the house and spread its front paws on her knees, a dog-smile on his face, just like his papa used to do. Jace's pickup roared up the road crunching gravel and came to a halt beside the house. He cut the engine then slid from behind the steering wheel. Marla hadn't expected him and anticipation took hold of her heart. The dog turned and loped down the steps to greet him.

"Evening, Marla," Jace said, rifling Little Buck's ears. "I think I left my hat here."

"Not unless Major ate it," Marla said with a grin.

"I suppose I could have left it somewhere else." Jace climbed the three flagstone steps to the porch, Little Buck at his heels. "I can see this pup's taken to you. Used to see ol' Buck when your dad took him hunting with my father. He was a real quail dog."

"The little guy's wonderful," Marla said with a smile.

Jace's "hat" excuse was pretty thinly veiled. If he wanted to see her, why didn't he call? But that wasn't his way. Marla waved her hand toward the chair beside her. "If you have a few minutes, why don't you take a seat?"

"Why not?" he replied.

Jace eased into the comfy chair and draped his lower leg over his other knee. In the last couple of weeks Marla had gotten to know Jace, the man, better. He was grounded and compassionate, with solid values. Everyone in the valley knew you could always call on the Van

Garretts in an emergency. She understood Jace was only trying to help her family, like he would anyone else's, yet she sensed there was something more going on between them, could feel it in her bones. Was he courting her in the old-fashioned way of their forebears? Certainly he was making excuses to see her every chance he got. An expectant tremor ran through her body.

Jace's gaze lingered on her figure as she rose and switched on the porch light. "You look very pretty tonight," he said. "I like the different colors of embroidery on the front of your blouse."

"Thanks. Mom embroidered it," Marla answered softly as she touched the drawstring around the top. It was an old cotton blouse she'd been thinking of tossing in the rag bag but his compliment changed her mind. She'd pulled her hair back and tied it with a blue ribbon. His admiring gaze made her feel quite feminine.

"Are your knees healing okay?" he asked.

"They're still a tiny bit sore but that won't last long," she said.

"Good."

Jace reached for her hand and examined each slim finger as though it was a precious gemstone. "You have beautiful hands," he said, his voice almost a whisper.

Embarrassed by her chipped fingernails, Marla pulled her hand away. He looked disappointed. "Thank you," she said. "I don't seem to have time to do things like manicures anymore."

"Don't worry about it. I meant what I said. My mom used to say you had a piano player's hands. You know, long tapering fingers for such a small gal."

Marla found herself giggling. All of a sudden, the necessity of going to a beauty salon seemed important. She could use a hair styling to get rid of split ends and have her fingernails shaped too. Still, she'd never admit it was Jace's showing an interest that made her think about these things.

"Going to the barn dance?" he asked, breaking into her thoughts. "I could pick you up."

She knew by the telltale sound of his voice he hoped she would say yes.

"I'm not sure," she said instead. "Things are so hectic here on the ranch right now."

His jaw tightened but he didn't push her. "Well, I better go find my hat."

Marla was disappointed. What had made her think he would beg her? Sure, he'd paid a little attention to her, but that didn't give her the right to feel so all-fired pompous.

Jace rose and stood over her. She didn't dare stand, lest she find herself in his arms, the urge being almost irresistible. "Goodnight," she said with a catch in her voice. "And I hope you find your hat."

A contemplative look came into his eyes. "See you around."

"Yeah."

Jace leaned over and lightly kissed her temple, then retraced his steps down the flagstones and got in the truck. Watching him drive away, Marla felt lonely. Why hadn't she been more talkative, more congenial, kept him there with her brilliant conversation? But she wasn't a woman who found small talk easy, and she certainly wasn't adept at flirting like her friend Judy. Judy could wrap a man around her little finger in two shakes, while

Marla stumbled over her words, ill at ease in the presence of a good-looking man.

The annual "Going Bullistic" rodeo opened with people coming from miles around. Marla, Judy and Debra sat in the grandstands watching the calf roping event. They jumped to their collective feet and shouted praise along with the crowd when Jace Van Garrett won the contest by two seconds. The featured bull riding event was next. Marla's chest tightened. Bull riding was a rough sport and riders often got hurt. She said a quiet prayer for Jace, along with the other participants.

Yet praying didn't alleviate Marla's concern for Jace. Darn it! Why couldn't he be happy winning the calf roping prize? No, he had to show he could ride one of those ornery bulls. She tried to calm down as the loudspeaker blared a song by Garth Brooks, her favorite singer, but not even he could keep her fear from working overtime.

The first rider, a baby-faced young man from Williams, managed to hang on to the rope for a few short seconds before being upended by the bull, along with his clean white hat. He barely missed landing on the bull's sharp horns. Everyone clapped for him when he scurried away from the angry beast.

Bull riding was being called the most exciting and fastest-growing spectator sport in the West. The winner of today's event would compete in Las Vegas at what was dubbed the "Super Bowl of rodeos."

Marla and her friends waited for the next rider's name to be announced. Marla closed her eyes and hoped it wouldn't be Jace.

"I think Jace is next," Judy said, excited.

Debra looked a little wild-eyed. "Oh, geez."

"I hope he doesn't break his darn-fool neck," Marla said.

"You know men. They're drawn to danger," Judy added. "It's in their genes."

Marla snapped her eyes shut just as Jace's number was called but opened them immediately. A crowd favorite, he climbed onto the fence railing beside the massive bull. Marla perched on the edge of the bleacher seat and balled her hands into white fists. He mounted the thunderous mass of solid beef, a gloved hand firmly securing the rope, the other free for balance.

In the next breathless moment, Jace nodded to the starter. The chute swung open and a hurricane of energy on four hoofs lunged toward the center of the arena. Jace Van Garrett held on for the bumpy thrill-ride. The massive bull snorted, shook and leaped without grace, its back legs shooting out like arrows toward the grandstand.

Marla sucked in her breath as the bull nearly stood on its head, electrifying the excited crowd and almost dislodging Jace. The force swung him back along the bull's backbone, while he tried to maintain his balance. Keeping his legs firmly around the animal's ribcage, he held on. The bull executed a quantum turn, almost spilling Jace on the ground, and spun in a circle two times like a child's top. Jace righted himself. Marla heard a gasp come from her own throat and her fist flew to her mouth.

The raucous throng jumped to its feet, roaring support. Marla didn't move an eyelash. Holding her breath for what had to be the longest eight seconds in her life, she sat statue rigid. Judy pulled on her arm but she scarcely noticed.

The buzzer fired away like a dentist's drill. Jace jumped down, landing on his feet. The clowns distracted the bull as Jace loped back to the gate. Marla let out her breath in a rush. Judy danced around her, whooping like a cheerleader.

"I wish Mom could have seen this," Debra said, her face alight.

"Me too," Marla said.

Other riders participated afterward but Jace's time held. Then the event was over. The announcer called Jace's name and time over the loudspeaker. Jace waved his arms in the air—the winner. Marla, Debra and Judy joined him in the arena, congratulating him and patting him on the shoulders. He held up his silver and turquoise trophy belt for everyone to see and the clapping grew deafening. Then he hugged his sister, Judy, and Marla.

"Jace," was all Marla could manage to say as she buried her face in his shoulder. Then she stepped back. "You darn fool. You're going to get yourself killed doing dumb stuff like that." She wiped away a tear, hoping he didn't notice it. Then the rodeo was over.

Marla braided her hair into a French braid. It heightened her cheekbones. She added lipstick and blush, cosmetics she rarely wore on the ranch, but wanted to look her best tonight. Jace had asked her to go to the barn dance with him but she'd decided to go with Judy, thinking it would be less complicated that way.

Marla left the house and strolled toward the Jeep in the barn, keys dangling from her hand. Twilight played on the old ranch buildings. All at once she experienced a creepy feeling, as though someone was watching her. She turned abruptly and glanced about, but there was no one in sight. The barn doors gaped open like a big black hole in outer space.

"Anyone there?" she called, grasping her keys in her hand.

A scratching sound came from within the barn and the tomcat wandered out, a dead mouse in its teeth. Marla grimaced. Inside the barn, darkness encircled as she jerked open the Jeep door. Climbing in, she started the engine and backed out of the big wooden doors.

Marla drove into town, her thoughts drifting back to Jace. Now that he was a rodeo winner, he'd be going to Las Vegas before long to compete in the annual event that drew thousands of people. Though terribly proud of him, she worried too. They didn't call bull riding an extreme sport for nothing. She recalled seeing a television documentary about a woman who had been mauled by a bull in Pamplona, Spain, during the running of the bulls. The enraged animal had tossed her about as though she were a Raggedy Ann doll, breaking practically every bone in the poor woman's body. She later died. The experience was enough to keep Marla a safe distance from bulls.

She parked in front of Judy's house and tooted the horn. Minutes later, they walked through the red barn doors and entered the festivities. Country and western music floated softly around them as Marla greeted old friends, Clyde and Janet Masterson. She spotted Jace heading toward the refreshment table with an attractive raven-haired woman dressed in a pretty long skirt that teased her ankles. The tunic the woman wore showed off her high bosom to best advantage.

Jace walked with the buoyancy of an athlete, all the while smiling at his companion. Marla's shoulders sagged as she wondered at the absurd feelings he generated in her, like this jealousy hovering around her now. Was Ms. Raven Hair his date? Had he asked the woman out of spite after Marla had turned him down?

Suddenly Marla didn't think she had dressed nice enough for the dance. The simple purple dress she wore seemed dated, her makeup too heavy. She thought about going into the restroom to wash it off, but changed her mind. She'd really look a mess then.

Judy drifted away with the Mastersons, leaving Marla standing alone just inside the entrance. From across the room, Jace craned his neck and glanced toward her, an unmistakable joy livening his face. He executed a quick maneuver to disengage himself from the woman, who turned to see where he was going. Marla was surprised to see Jill, his cousin, which caused her to feel sheepish. *Duh*! she told herself. Jill tossed Marla a friendly wave and Marla waved back. Jace cut through the dancers to reach her.

Judy danced by with Tom Alden, a young man she currently had a giant crush on. His father was the local judge. Tom, however, hadn't gotten his feet set firmly on the ground yet.

Then Jace was standing in front of Marla. "Want to dance?" he asked, his mouth working into a devastating smile.

"That sounds like a winner," she said, returning his smile.

Chapter Ten

"You were great today," Marla said when Jace took her hand.

"Nice of you to say so," he said, eyes twinkling. He pulled her into his arms and they joined the dancers. She focused on the three-piece band across the room, wanting to escape the intense gaze he gave her, though it thrilled her down to her toes.

"I'd have gladly picked you up tonight," he said.

"Judy doesn't have any wheels. Her truck broke down," she said by way of an excuse.

"Uh huh. I could have picked you both up," he insisted.

Marla didn't reply. Jace was quick and light on his feet, and Marla felt good in his embrace, if a mite confused by the excitement playing with her thought processes.

"Tell me, weren't you a little bit frightened of that crazy bull?" she asked, shifting subjects.

"I'd be crazy not to be, but riding it was a heck of a lot of fun, all the same."

"You men—always testing yourselves. Still, I'm glad you didn't get hurt."

"Don't you worry about me, hon."

"I wasn't worried," she fibbed, thinking he must know she wasn't telling the truth, her face an open book.

"I looked for you when I got here and was disappointed when I didn't see you," he said. "I thought you might not show."

"Oh?"

"Yeah." A sensuous light played around his eyes. The music ended, followed by another sweet Western tune. He led her to the center of the barn. "I like those little dangly earrings you're wearing," he said, and reached up to touch the tiny silver coyotes.

Marla's face heated as she thanked him. His palm slid around her back and rested in the small of her spine as he wrapped her hand in his free one, his liquid dark eyes focusing directly on her lips. His nearness caused her body to tingle and she felt as though her brain was short-circuiting to mush. Their eyes met in a tantalizing moment that made her feel giddy all over.

"Tell me more about that bull ride," she said, clearing her throat. "Now you'll be hurrying off to Las Vegas, I suppose. Wish I could be there to see you compete."

"Hey, why couldn't you come along? Mom and Debra plan to go."

Marla shied away from accepting. "I've got loads to do here with Dad in a fix. You know that."

"Mm, but you've got Hull now—the 'important' trainer."

"We'll see."

"Well, it won't keep me from hoping."

The more she thought about going, the more she wanted to. "It would be fun," Marla admitted.

"You'll go," he said, his eyes glowing.

Caught up in the music, Marla smiled as they flowed among the dancers. She enjoyed the bold strength of Jace's arms around her and the non-verbal clues he sent. Jace wasn't hiding his desire for her, and she didn't quite know how to handle the situation.

While he held her closer, she could almost feel the beat of his heart through his shirt. Then he spun her out to the rhythm of the music before reeling her in so close her body hugged his firm torso. His square jaw rested against the crown of her hair and she breathed in his uniquely masculine scent mingled with aftershave and leather. She tried to breathe normally but her heart kept pounding in an abnormal rhythm.

Marla had to admit she'd become increasingly attracted to Jace's charismatic charms, though she never intended to act on those feelings.

The song ended and Marla breathed a shaky sigh of relief. However, like a possessive lover, Jace kept her hand firmly enfolded in his. "Let's go outside and get some fresh air," he said.

Marla nodded. "It's so hot," she said, fanning herself.

They strolled among the parked cars. "It's much nicer out here," Jace said. He let go of her hand as he leaned against a fender, crossed his arms over his chest, and glanced upward. The sky was ablaze with diamond-studded stars and the moon shimmered like a pewter globe. Speaking in a soft cadence, he asked her about herself. "You getting back into the swing of ranch life after being away so long?"

Marla locked her hands behind her back. "I'm trying to." She hesitated before adding, "I've been waiting to hear whether I'll be hired for the fall school session in Flagstaff, and now I'm in a quandary. With Dad injured, I won't be able to take the offer."

Jace crimped his mouth. Then he asked a question that caused her mind to lurch. "Why don't you teach right here in Coyote Springs?"

Marla gulped. "Like in *Little House on the Prairie?*"

"Why not? You could be both teacher and principal, like Eleanor Harper used to be. She was happy enough until she married and moved to San Diego. Heck, there's a lot of kids in this valley and it'll be a real shame if they have to be bussed all the way to Flagstaff. They won't be able to participate in any after school extracurricular activities like sports and 4-H."

Marla stared back at Jace in surprise. He looked dead serious. "You're forgetting the school's closed," she said.

He didn't bat an eyelash. "We'll reopen it. Seems to me we only need a qualified teacher."

"I'm astonished you'd even think I could do it. I'm a new teacher," she reminded him. "Have you any idea of the red tape that would be involved?"

"You want to teach, right? These kids need a teacher. It's as simple as that."

Her stomach did a somersault. "I'm not sure I could accomplish everything—teaching and acting as the principal. Besides, time's running out."

His eyes crinkled into a smile and he reached over and took both her hands in his. "Think about it, hon. I'll back you all the way with the school board."

"But it would be a monumental task," she exclaimed with a nervous laugh. "Moreover, I doubt I'd be qualified to take the position. They'd never hire an inexperienced teacher in a million years."

Jace released Marla's hands and stood up straight, towering over her. "C'mon, sunshine, give it a try. 'Nothing ventured, nothing gained,' as the old saying goes."

She pursed her mouth. "Of course I'll think about it, but . . ."

"Hey, you can do it. I know you. You're adventurous, always daring, and uh, sometimes reckless."

She laughed. "You're exaggerating all over the place."

Jace laughed too, then switched topics. "I was wondering if you saved that last dance for me."

"I haven't forgotten," Marla said, still perplexed over what Jace had said. He'd opened a can of worms, then let the matter drop like a hot skillet.

"Then let's dance."

"The evening's not nearly over," she reminded him.

"We'll pretend every dance is the last, and I've got dibs on all of them."

Marla chuckled as he took her hand in his in the moonlight, feeling overwhelmed as he guided her through the parking lot. Inside the barn, she laid her head under his chin as they danced. He hummed the words to the country-and-western song and she couldn't help feel that what they were sharing was terribly romantic.

Jace and Marla danced the entire evening as though

they were the only ones on the dance floor. She couldn't remember having so much fun. He was witty and charming—an engaging partner.

"Can I take you home?" he asked when the music died away and the trio of musicians began to put their instruments away.

Marla wished she could say yes, but circumstances got in the way. "I pickcd up Judy, remember?" she said with a gentle reminder.

"Oh." Jace sounded disappointed.

"Thanks, anyway. I had a good time," Marla said, though she wanted to say a *wonderful* time.

Jace walked her to the refreshment table, poured lemonade into plastic glasses, and handed one to her. "Cheers," he said, holding his glass up.

Marla chuckled. Jace had a quixotic humor that didn't fail to amuse her. She'd forgiven him for treating her like a teenager, and he was most assuredly treating her like a real woman tonight.

Judy joined them, her lips pulled down at the corners. "Why does the dance have to end so early? It's only midnight."

"Rules," Jace said, though he looked equally sad.

"There'll be other dances," Marla said, letting her face glow as Jace smiled down at her.

He walked them to Marla's Jeep and said goodnight, then strolled away into the darkness. Marla dropped Judy off at her house. Along the quiet stretch of highway to the ranch, Marla's thoughts were a dizzy jumble. She recalled the clever things Jace had said, his mannerisms. Coupled with the attention he'd shown her, it caused her heart to race all over again. She asked herself if they could possibly build a real relationship. Both were strong-willed, determined people. Then she spotted car lights far behind her and wondered if it was Jace seeing her safely home. The speculation caused her to grin.

Marla rose after the rooster's first sharp crow and dressed in jeans and a cotton lace-trimmed tank top. She cleaned the house, then drove into town to grocery shop for her mother. Carrying her list, she hurried inside the market. Debra, Jace's sister, nearly collided with her when they both turned a corner between the packaged dinners and juice.

"Say, are you going to a race, my friend?" Debra asked with a grin.

"Sorry. I had other things on my mind."

Debra rounded her pretty almond-shaped eyes. "Have a good time at the barn dance last night?"

"You talked to Jace?"

"No. Mr. Closed Mouth wouldn't tell me anything, but Judy called."

"Judy likes to embellish things. But, yeah, I had a nice time," she admitted. "Jace and I danced some."

"Judy said you didn't dance with anyone else."

"Judy talks too much."

Debra chuckled. "Do you like Jace a little more now that you're all grown up?"

"Really, Debra, you make it sound like we're teen-agers again. He's nice enough."

Debra shrugged. "Have it your way, Marla. Well, I've got to get outa' here. Only stopped in for their special dog food. Mom's Lab has stomach trouble."

Marla smiled. "I adore her puppy. Oh, and tell Mary I'll drop by real soon and bring Mom along with me."

"She'll look forward to it."

On the way home, Marla stopped at the school and walked slowly through the deserted, weed-infested playground, thinking of all the children who would normally be playing come fall. But not this year. She rested on her heels and tried to resurrect her own days as a student there, the fun and activities. It brought a sudden smile to her lips. Could she even hope to teach here? Returning to the Jeep, she sat for awhile before starting the engine and thought about what Jace had said the night before. Surely his idea had to be crazy.

Two days later, Marla and her mother visited Mary Van Garrett and her daughter. The older women were long-time friends. The Van Garrett ranch was well cared for, the main house and outbuildings newly painted. A windbreak of cottonwood trees surrounded the house, keeping down the dust. Horses nodded sleepily in the pasture.

"Coffee's ready," Mary said to her guests as they stood in the kitchen. "We'll take our cups into the living room."

They accompanied her along the uncluttered travel pattern back to the great room. Well-worn leather sofas flanked either side of the river-rock fireplace. A box of toys and books were stacked neatly on a wicker tea table beside the hearth. Mary had needlepointed flowery pillows for the sofas before she'd gone blind and they still looked fresh and new.

Marla and her mother sat on a sofa. "I've been wanting to stop by and say hello for ages," JoAnn said. "I haven't seen you since Charlie got hurt." She inhaled the coffee's pleasant aroma. "It didn't take long before he was on a first name basis with most of the nurses at the hospital, though I suspect they were glad to see him leave. He's home now, thanks to the screws in his leg."

"Good. I'm glad to have you both here," Mary said, "and hope Charlie heals real fast."

"It was awful," JoAnn said. "I was afraid he might be bedridden the rest of his life. That would have killed him." She shook her head. "Wish he'd give up roping, but you know how stubborn he is."

"I'm afraid Dad has a mind of his own," Marla interjected.

"That's so typical of men. They always have to prove themselves," Mary said with a little smile.

The coffee's steam rose temptingly and Marla took a sip. Mary passed the banana bread she'd baked with Debra's help. Mary's skill always amazed Marla. An attractive woman in her mid fifties, she had retained her slim figure with only a hint of thickness around the waist. She'd pulled back her dark, shiny hair into a neat ponytail and fastened it with a silver clip. Only a few streaks of gray were evident. Though blind and widowed, she was a strong woman who rarely showed any sign of sorrow.

Mary reached out like a homing pigeon and patted Marla's shoulder. "I understand you're going to be teaching here in our community. I can't tell you how relieved that makes me feel—you taking over. Just think of it."

Marla nearly choked on the next swallow of coffee, feeling the heat rip down her throat. JoAnn spoke up. "You okay, hon?"

Marla got herself under control. "Did Jace tell you that?" Marla asked Mary, trying to contain her shock.

Mary frowned. "Oh, dear, did Jace let the cat out of the bag?"

"What's this all about?" JoAnn cut in. "You don't tell me anything."

"Seems Jace is putting the cart before the horse," Marla said. "He only made the suggestion at the barn dance the other night. Frankly, I didn't take him seriously." She spread her hands on her lap after setting the cup on a tray.

"I thought the school was closed," JoAnn said.

"Right, and the powers that be aren't likely to reopen it, let alone for someone inexperienced like me to run the place."

"But you practiced teaching all last year," JoAnn reminded her. "It's not as though you don't have any experience."

"That's hardly the same, Mom."

"You'd be a wonderful teacher," Mary said.

"If only you could," Debra added. "I hate to think of my kids having to take the bus all that way."

"Besides, there's the ranch to run," Marla said, trying to keep the wistfulness from her voice.

JoAnn spoke. "We've hired a trainer. He'll certainly make things easier on us until your dad is better."

Mary looked keenly at Marla, as though she could see as well as anyone. "About teaching, it's important to follow your goals, Marla, dear. With a new trainer, you ought to be able to take any teaching assignment offered."

Marla thought about what Mary said. "Things are still

iffy in that department. I don't think it's wise to go away just yet. As for the school, well . . ."

"I understand," Mary said. "It was a nice thought, anyway."

Marla picked up the cup and smoothed her hands around it. They launched into talking about church, Debra's pregnancy, and the drought, then said good-bye.

Across the barnyard, Marla saw Jace giving Adam, Debra's son, a ride on his horse. The boy sat snugly against his uncle as Jace's gray gelding trotted in a circle in the corral. When Jace looked up and saw Marla, she threw him a toss of the hand. Jace nodded in recognition, keeping his attention on the boy. She climbed into the Jeep with her mother and put the key in the ignition. Mary and Debra stood on the porch. Marla wished she could be as serene about her own life as Mary Van Garrett. A quiet woman, she was every inch a survivor.

An early morning breeze fluttered the bedroom curtains like a sea of new wheat. Marla sat up and yawned. She had been laying there thinking for the past hour. Time was running out for any plans to reopen the school. Could Jace really be serious? The whole thing seemed impossible. And Jace Van Garrett? He was stirring up a heap of sensuous thoughts in her head, though she tried to keep a lid on them. Going on twenty-five, she wasn't involved in any kind of relationship. However, most of her friends, with the exception of Judy, were already married.

Marla groaned. No job, no man, no marriage, no children. Nothing. She had traditional values, and the right man was very important to her plans, but at this point her future had hit a dead end.

With the trainer on the ranch, she might be able to go away to teach the second semester. Yet, that meant she wouldn't see much of Jace, and his suggestion about the school was nothing more than a pipe dream.

Marla swung her legs from the bed, stood on the cowhide rug, scrunched her toes in the brown fur, and took a couple of deep breaths. She crossed the hardwood floor to the chest of drawers and peered at her reflection in the mirror above it. She'd dropped a few pounds in the months since returning home and her cheeks looked hollow, pale circles under her eyes. She pushed back her sleep-tousled hair and ran a palm over her cheekbone. Would things get better anytime soon?

Marla tossed the white cotton nightgown she'd worn over a chair-back and showered quickly, then picked up a wide-toothed brush and combed her hair.

Downstairs in the kitchen, Marla thought about Jace's call the night before. He'd encouraged her to contact the county school district. Didn't he realize the authorities would never consider her for a position in Coyote Springs? The last thing she wanted was to cheat children out of a good education, yet she had confidence in her abilities. Her grades in college had been excellent. One of her professors had even told her she was a born teacher. However, here in the valley she'd have no one above her to go to with a problem, even if they considered her offer.

Marla took down a box of Kashi from the cupboard, poured milk in a bowl and ate, hardly tasting the cereal. Operation overload was taking its toll on her. She ought to be out in the corral working with the yearlings by this time instead of just getting herself together.

Marla found Grant Hull in the stable office. "Is everything going okay?" she asked. "Settling in?"

Hull nodded. "Can't complain." He folded a stick of mint gum in his mouth and chewed. A tattoo on his forearm looked like a scorpion or was it a seahorse?

Marla took a seat behind her father's scarred metal desk and gave Hull a closer look as he gathered himself up to speak. The man could talk your leg off or be as silent as a tomb. He had a shovel jaw and chin, his lower lip extended over the upper one. Most of the time he breathed through his mouth, as though he had an adenoid problem, and his forehead slanted toward a Dick Tracy nose. When he smiled, his eyes remained hard. She couldn't quite figure him out. However, if he proved to be a good trainer, she didn't care about the rest.

"As I see it, you're short hands," Hull said, parking his rump on the edge of the desk. "But we won't worry about it right now. By the way, I'm beginning to like that bay yearling you call Major. Smart as a whip. Going to be invaluable with livestock, though it took me a while to get him to come around."

Marla thought of how Jace had handled Major. "Well, the horse will go up for sale soon enough," she said. "He ought to bring in a good price."

Hull scratched his jaw. "Might buy him off you, myself."

For some reason, Marla wasn't sure she wanted to sell the yearling to him. "We'll see. Actually, Jace Van Garrett has shown an interest." She brought her hands together, forming a church with a steeple.

Hull began to ramble about his past successes. "Don't think I'm bragging," he said, "but I want you to understand I have a lot of experience with cutting horses, and experience counts in this business."

"Yes," Marla said. Suddenly she felt bored and wished he'd leave the office and let her get the bookkeeping done. She took a ledger from a drawer and laid it on the desktop, opening it. When Hull didn't get up, she said, "The horses have to be ready soon, so I'm counting on you. We have that deadline we talked about."

"Anything I can do, just let me know," Hull said affably. Then he launched into some ideas he had about improving the stables. "Those new automatic feeders we used in Florida worked just fine. They have a new one that does a better job of filtering out the bugs in the troughs." He glanced around, his eyes widening. "Ms. Shelton, this place could be a first class operation with a little money and additional hired hands."

"We don't have that kind of money," Marla said.

When she didn't show any enthusiasm, he blew out his cheeks. "I'll be on my way now but you just yell if there's anything at all you want done."

Hull lumbered away, heading toward the bunkhouse. Marla sighed with relief. She liked some of his ideas but they spelled big bucks. Maybe later they could afford to make some changes but not at the moment. She debated whether to discuss it with Jace, but knew what he'd probably say. "You don't spend money out of an empty wagon," or something like that. And their alfalfa fields were drying up faster than overcooked rice. Who knew when the drought would end? A bird in hand was worth two in the bush, her grandmother used to say, and she was a wise woman. Marla tried not to look too far into the future for fear of seeing something bad, like losing the ranch.

Chapter Eleven

In the stableyard, Jeff Begay bent to trim one of the horse's hooves. Marla sauntered over to him, thinking how gentle and efficient he was with them.

"Hey," she said. "Need some help?"

Jeff turned his head toward her. "Nah," he said, then lowered the horse's foot. His forehead furrowed when he muttered something, the words so low Marla didn't catch them.

"What's up?" she asked, sensing the young man wasn't his usual friendly self.

"I'll get my things when I finish here," he said with a dour expression. "But it'll be a day or two before I can find another stable for my horse. Hope you don't mind if I leave him here."

Marla's mind reeled. "What are you talking about?"

"Hull fired me. Didn't he tell you?"

"Just wait a darn minute," Marla said, placing hands on hips. "You're not going anywhere. Dad and I do the hiring and firing around here. You're a good worker and I'm not about to let you go. By the way, where's Hull?"

Jeff looked skeptical. "Like usual, he's probably takin' another of his siestas behind the barn. In all honesty, Marla, the man disappears nearly as soon as you're out of sight and leaves me to do most of the work. Heck, I don't mind workin' with the horses, never have, but Hull turns around and takes the credit, his chest all stuck out like he has medals on it. Reads me the riot act about every little thing, too. Galls me something awful. If he's an authority on cutting horses, my dog's president of these United States. And the man shows no patience with the yearlings."

"Why didn't you tell me about this?"

"It would have been his word against mine. Besides, I hoped he'd up and leave, since he doesn't seem very satisfied. Wishful thinking, I guess."

Shocked by this revelation, Marla said, "I'm really sorry about all this, Jeff. Of course you can stay on."

His mouth worked. "Things came to a head this morning. We nearly came to blows when he hit Major with his fist for not standing still when he was saddling him. Hull said, 'I'm goin'a straighten this colt out once and for all.' Yearlings get spooked easy. Anyone with any sense knows that. I guess I would have quit anyway, even if he hadn't given me the ax."

Marla bit her lower lip and took in a deep breath before expelling it in anger. "You can't go, Jeff. We need you. I'll handle this. You sit tight. And thanks for being honest. I've been awfully preoccupied with things. Sorry."

"I'm not blaming you," Jeff said, hope shining in his

eyes. "Maybe I ought to come along if you're going to talk to Hull."

"No need. I'll make this quick." Although Hull wasn't Hannibal Lecter, what she'd learned scared her all the same. You couldn't trust a person who'd be mean to an animal. But this was her responsibility.

"Much obliged," Jeff said.

"Sure." She turned on her heel and stomped away. Fire spewed in every nerve in her body. The more she thought about how she'd been taken in, the more incensed she became. The audacity of that man!

Marla had noticed other things that irritated her, such as equipment left carelessly laying around. Then she'd noticed one of the yearlings had a two inch strip of hide removed on the rump. Hull explained it away by saying one of the horses nipped the other, but it didn't look like a bite mark. And why hadn't she seen how tired Jeff looked? With an extra man on the ranch, his load should have been lighter. Guilt wove it's way to consciousness as she thought about these things.

Marla headed for the barn and marched around the side. Normally, there was nothing behind the building but an open field full of tumbleweeds and sandburs that needed to be cleared away. She found Hull sleeping in a lounge chair he'd apparently brought from storage and positioned in the shade. Broad-brimmed hat pulled low over his forehead, he'd crossed his arms over his chest. He snored in a gulp of air and it rattled in his throat. She smelled the unmistakable odor of stale booze on his breath and her temper rose. Now she knew why he chewed so many sticks of gum.

"Hull!" she thundered.

He barely stirred. She bent and shook his shoulder vigorously.

Hull's eyes snapped open like a doll's and he unfolded his arms, his hat falling to the ground. His expression turned to cold stone. "What in tarnation?" he muttered.

"You're supposed to be working," she said, her voice rife with authority.

Hull managed to get on his feet. "You begrudge a hardworking man a little nap, lady?" he said in defense. "Got something against working folks?"

Frustration welled inside Marla. "I've heard about your little naps!"

A sardonic look wafted across Hull's face. "You been listening to that lazy whelp of an Indian?"

"Jeff never lies and he's not lazy, either."

"I canned the mouthy kid!" he boomed. "I'm the trainer and you gave me permission to run this place as I see fit." His eyes darted past her. "What's he still doing on the place, away? I told him to clear out."

Marla had all she could do to keep from screaming at the rude, insufferable slob. "You had no right to fire Jeff. We own this place, not you. Jeff stays. You go. Got it? I want you to be gone by the end of the week."

Hull's mouth turned zipper thin and a strange flicker came into his eyes. Alone with him, the unexpected realization struck Marla like a bolt that he might try to harm her. She stiffened.

In a flash, Hull reached out and grabbed her forearm in a vice-like grip. The carotid artery in his neck vibrated as he gave her a humorless laugh. Trapped, she felt as frightened as a field mouse clutched in a chicken hawk's beak.

"Let go of me, you idiot!" Marla barked with all the courage she could muster.

Hull squeezed harder, making her flinch. "You're not firing me, girlie. You better see the handwriting on the wall. I'm boss now and I'm staying or there'll be triple-duty consequences, like your old man's other leg getting broke."

"Are you threatening us?" Her voice jumped up the scales.

Hull shrugged. "Take it for what it is."

She wrenched free. "And you take this for what it is. You've go twenty-four hours to clear off this ranch, hear?"

Hull made another move toward Marla. For a moment she felt uncertainty take hold of her, along with growing fright. Jeff suddenly appeared from around the building carrying a shovel. "Everything okay here, Marla?" he asked.

Hull lurched off, cursing the wind.

At first Marla thought she wouldn't tell Jace she'd had words with Grant Hull, thinking he'd only say, "See, I told you so." Besides, Hull would soon be gone. But her better judgment prevailed. She'd come to care for Jace and needed his sound advice and emotional support.

Later, Marla met him for lunch at Molly's Coffee Shoppe and they ordered tuna sandwiches. She was grateful for all he'd done. Sitting across from him, she thought about how their relationship had taken a subtle change. He had a kind of sweetness in his nature under all the masculine bravura. It, too, attracted him to her.

"How are things going at the ranch?" he asked, holding his gaze on her. "Hull doing his job?"

Could he read her mind? "Things aren't too bad. Dad's better. That's a relief. But . . ."

When she paused, he said, "And?"

"I fired Hull."

"You what . . . ?" His eyes widened. "What happened?"

She told him part of it but not about the trainer's trying to man-handle her.

"I never liked him. Too shifty-eyed," Jace said.

"But Dad has already countermanded me." She also hadn't told her father about Hull's reaction, afraid his anger might give him a heart attack.

Jace's eyebrows flew together. "Why would Charlie do that?"

"Because we've got to get those horses ready by the deadline or we won't be able to pay our taxes. That's the way it is, I'm afraid. We couldn't find a replacement at this late date."

"I could talk to Charlie."

"It wouldn't do any good. And he's right."

Marla could tell by Jace's expression he didn't like it but there was nothing he could do. He sat there a moment then changed the subject. "Have you given the school any more thought?"

She wet her lower lip. "Actually, that's why I invited you to lunch."

He gave her a quizzical look. "It isn't every day a beautiful woman asks a guy like me to have lunch. Even went to the trouble to change my boots." Letting a grin spread across his face, he took a long drink of iced tea.

Marla glanced down. He had his fancy leather rodeo boots on. "I do want to teach here in Coyote Springs," she said. "It seems all wrong, those kids stuffed in a smelly bus five days a week. And I know I could do it. Well, I think so . . ." Her words ran together in her haste to get them out. "But getting approval is something else. Frankly, it seems overwhelming."

Jace didn't speak for a moment, absorbed in what she'd told him. Then he leaned back in the chair across from her. "That's what I wanted to hear," he said with enthusiasm. "So you'll do it?"

"Yes." She sighed.

Customers turned to stare at them, their ears pricked, waiting to hear some juicy gossip. Jace bent forward. "You're serious now, babe? You won't back down?"

"Don't call me babe." Marla turned and glared at the customers watching them. They quickly found other things of interest to look at. She swung back to Jace. "Of course I'm serious. I said it, didn't I? But I don't see how . . ."

Picking up on her nervousness, he wiped a smile from his face. "You realize, it'll be all over town the minute after we walk out of here?"

Marla sighed. "I know this town's grapevine only too well." She paused before going on. "I called the district office this morning, as you advised. They didn't sound too encouraging but asked me to send a copy of my credential and resume. I did it on the way here. And I have an appointment tomorrow morning to meet with the Superintendent of Public Instruction."

He rewarded her with a broad smile. "Wow! You're way ahead of me. I'll drive you over to Flagstaff. I know the school board will be in favor of what you've decided. Say, this is a cause to celebrate. Heck, I'll even pay for your lunch."

Marla laughed. "You may not be so joyous when I tell you what I want you to do. I dropped by the school the other day. The place looks pretty run-down. It will take a lot of work. That is, if I even get the job."

"Mm."

"Among other things, it hasn't been painted in years."

"You want me to paint the building?"

"You got it. School can't open with dirty walls, poor plumbing, and gummy desks."

Jace scratched his ear. "We get the okay, I'll be there, and with the paint. Call it a donation."

After lunch, they walked to Marla's Jeep. Jace insisted on holding her hand. People around town would have something else to talk about if he didn't stop being so attentive. But Marla knew Jace all too well. He was a touchy-feely guy. It was just the way he was, and he didn't mean anything by it. But no wonder so many of the women around had their hats set for him. As for Marla, she didn't have time to think of romance. If her proposal to take over the school went through, she'd be up to her ankles in preparations and meetings. The problem with Hull only magnified everything. She probably wouldn't get any more work out of him, and how was she going to fill his job?

Marla had slept little when the alarm assailed her ears. She sat up, her thoughts a continuation of her doubts the night before. What made her think she had a chance to get the school reopened? Jace, however, had assured her the townsfolk would volunteer to fill in when she needed them. Oh, he was persuasive, all right.

Marla rolled off the bed and took a couple of deep breaths to clear her head. Jace would pick her up in an hour. The decision having been made to go for it, she felt happy, even exuberant about reopening the old school. Did she really have a chance? The school authorities had agreed to at least listen to her proposition.

Marla crossed the floor and stuck her head in the closet. This meeting called for something more than blue jeans and a tank top. She decided on a pale blue dress and a multicolored vest. The boots could stay at home.

After a quick shower, she brushed her hair and finished dressing. Jace's truck rolled to a stop in front of the house just as she stepped onto the porch. Producing a warm smile, he opened the truck door for her.

"You look pretty with your hair down," he said, his voice brimming with enthusiasm. "Hey, this is going to be your lucky day, sunshine."

"I wish I had your confidence," Marla said, then thanked him for the compliment. She slid in, attached the seat belt, and placed the portfolio of documents she'd brought along on her lap.

They arrived late to the meeting due to heavy traffic. Marla felt a touch of panic as they took the elevator to the second floor. It wasn't the elevator that made her short of breath, it was meeting the Superintendent of Schools face to face. She hoped she wouldn't act like a wimp and show how vulnerable she felt. What made her think she had a chance, even if Jace came along as her cheerleader? *Come on,* she told herself. *You can't let self doubt defeat you before you even get going. Shape up, girl.*

In the superintendent's outer office, Marla fidgeted in the chair beside Jace. He looked handsome in Dockers and a button-down shirt. Though he'd set aside his Wrangler jeans, he hadn't set aside his Stetson and boots.

The middle-aged secretary behind the desk spoke. "Could I get you a cup of coffee? It's fresh."

"No, thanks," Marla said, thinking she couldn't possibly swallow coffee in her tense state. She glanced at Jace, who took the woman up on the offer. He looked cool and in control.

Five minutes later, Marla and Jace were ushered into the superintendent's office, its Navajo white walls covered with certificates and plaques. They exchanged handshakes, then sat down across the desk from Mr. Jennings. He grabbed Marla's curiosity the moment she saw him. Short and undistinguished-looking, he didn't appear to be the stereotypical superintendent. Jennings' complexion was florid and he had a cherub's bow mouth. Wisps of thin hair partly covered his head.

Realizing she had only nanoseconds to make her point, Marla scarcely paused to organize her thoughts, before launching in eagerly. "We're excited about the possibility of keeping our school open this fall," she said. "It means a lot to the local children and their parents. We can have a fine little school if you'll only give us permission to move ahead."

Jennings nodded without commenting. Marla knew she had to hook the man like Ernest Hemingway's big fish in *The Old Man and the Sea*, if she was to convince him of her sincerity. That meant making him understand she was a "can do" woman. "I already have several volunteers lined up for the reading program and sports activities." She gestured toward Jace. "He'll be the acting coach."

Jace beamed. He'd been sitting there letting her have her say, giving an occasional encouraging mutter. "The local school board backs Marla all the way," he answered.

"I see," Jennings said. "Haven't we met?"

"At a fund-raiser," Jace said, his eyes widening. "It was very successful."

"Ah, now I remember." Jennings turned back to Marla but didn't give anything away. Folding his hands in his lap, he said, "You're contemplating quite an undertaking, Ms. Shelton. Do you realize just what all this would entail? Summer's nearly over and the schools will open in a matter of weeks."

"I know I can do it," Marla said with enthusiasm. "The town will back me 100 percent."

"Yes. I did hear from the chairman of the school board."

Marla explained how she would go about running the school. The superintendent's face took on a skeptical look that caused her to question whether she was getting through to him.

After hearing her proposal, Jennings leaned closer. "How would you handle the various grades so that each student received an equivalent amount of time?" he asked.

"I would work with two grades at a time while other children worked on projects in their workbooks or on the computers. Volunteers will be there to help every morning."

"Computers? My, I don't think we could come up with

funds, since every penny has pretty much been earmarked for other things."

"We'll get them somehow," she said, straightening in the chair.

Marla wondered if all this sounded logical to the man. Without commenting further on the computers, Jennings asked questions about her teacher training. She handed over the portfolio with the transcripts, diploma, and the grades received when she worked that last year as a teacher's assistant. He scanned them.

Jennings cleared his throat and glanced up over his eyeglasses. "These look favorable. Frankly, I'm impressed, young woman."

"Thank you. I'm confident I can bring this all together, if you give me the opportunity," she said. "And I'll be armed with an excellent math program I found on the internet."

"Oh?"

"The children can ask questions and get answers in a timely fashion. If it meets with your approval, that is."

"Where would you get computers?" he asked, raising his eyebrows.

"I plan to donate one and Jace said he'd donate another," she interjected, tossing her head Jace's way. He nodded. "The church said they'd donate, too, along with the Cattlemen's Assocation. The Women's Club offered, as well."

These were some of the things Jace had done behind her back and only told her about on the way to Flagstaff. Marla could tell by the superintendent's expression he liked the idea.

"I see you've done your homework," Jennings said.

"This would be a sort of expanded home teaching, I take it."

She wasn't sure he liked that and phrased her next words carefully. "We'd be under the control of the local school board, sir, as well as the county and state."

Jace resettled his body in the chair and cut in before Jennings could comment. "My grandparents attended a one room school house and got a reasonably good education, enough that my grandfather went on to college and became a county supervisor."

Jennings tossed Jace an amiable smile. "Commendable. But there is so much more to learn these days."

"That's where computers come in," Jace said.

Marla dived back in. "With a TV, I can show them the world. There are excellent travelogues, programs on wildlife, and history. But our approach would very much be hands-on."

Jennings scratched his head. Marla finished her presentation, took a deep breath, and hoped the man would look favorably on her plans.

"I like your enthusiasm and your progressive ideas," Jennings said after a moment. "I'll take it to the board and see what they think."

Marla and Jace thanked the superintendent for his time and left the office. She felt like she had mental indigestion. "Do you think he'll decide in our favor?" she asked, hanging on to what seemed like a slim chance when all was said and done.

"Of course, hon. You impressed the heck out of me, surging through the whole deal like an army of ants. Jennings couldn't possibly miss that. My guess is he'll jump at the chance. Saves the school district a bundle on transportation alone, considering the price of gasoline these days."

"I wish I was as sure as you are, Jace. If Jennings does say yes, you realize I'll have to prove to the community I can do it, as well. But most of all, I don't want to fail the children."

Jace reached over and cupped her chin. "It's not in your makeup to fail anyone. Don't you worry now."

The next few days dragged on with agonizing slowness as Marla waited to be notified about whether she'd be hired and the school reopened. Then the call came through, along with the payoff.

"I like your drive and your ideas," Mr. Jennings said. "I'm going to take a chance on you. Now don't let me down."

"Why, I . . . " she said, fumbling her words. "Thanks. You won't be sorry."

"I see no plausible reason not to give the okay, since there is already a school there in Coyote Springs. You'll receive official notification through the mail. And we've contacted the local school board. They think it's a grand idea. But you do realize you have a deadline? School will open the day after Labor Day. Can you draw all the threads together that soon?"

"Of course I can, and I'll get on it right away," Marla said. Actually, she wasn't sure of anything. There'd be no time for putzing around, no procrastinating.

"Good luck then, Ms. Shelton," Jennings said in a cordial voice.

Marla replaced the receiver. Counting down the minutes, she flew through the screen door and raced to the barn. Unaware of the cat sleeping on the cushion beside her, she jammed the key in the Jeep's ignition and started the engine. The cat raised its head and let out a yowl. Marla quickly removed him. He jumped on a bale of hay and glared at her as she backed out, careful the puppy wasn't in the way. Hunching forward, Marla raced down the bumpy road toward Jace's ranch, eager to share the news with him personally.

A trail of dust behind the Jeep announced her arrival. Marla parked and climbed out, scarcely able to contain herself. She found Jace in the barn tinkering with a tractor. "Jace," she cried. "Guess what?"

A streak of grease creased one of his eyebrows. He set the hammer he'd been using on a wooden countertop and wiped his hands on a stained cloth, then picked up his hat and sat it on the back of his head. "Wasn't expecting you," he said, his eyes lighting.

"I got hired," she said, breathless.

Jace swung her around, then set her on her feet. "I didn't doubt it for a minute." His face worked into a broad grin. "You're right for it."

They hurried inside the house to share the good news with Mary, his mother.

Jace's encourgement had made Marla feel empowered, as well as determined to enrich the children's young lives. Thirty-six children, in grades first through eighth, were scheduled to enroll.

Jace met Marla at the school the following day. She unlocked the double doors and stood back, the musty smells of the closed building assailing her.

"I haven't been in this place since I graduated from

the eighth grade," she said in wonder, peering around at the dull walls.

Jace smiled and hauled in two big pails of paint he'd brought along.

"White, with a dollop of peach mixed in," he said, glancing at the label. "Just what you ordered."

"Perfect. It will give these institutional walls a hint of sunshine."

Jace tossed Marla a generous smile. She liked his openness and his being willing to help her. They walked back to the Jeep and unloaded the ladders, drop cloths, brushes, and assorted items.

"Where do you want to start?" Jace asked. He wore cutoffs and a faded blue T-shirt, minus the arms. Even in grubby clothes, he looked good, his well-toned muscles on display.

"Let's see for starters." She looked around.

Jace rubbed his unshaven jaw. "I thought maybe I could get some of the ranch hands over here but darn if they weren't all knee-deep in work."

"Oh, no you don't," she said. "You're the guy who volunteered, and I'm holding your to your promise." Then she laughed, realizing he was putting her on.

A man used to taking control, Jace said, "We'll begin in the main room, then work our way through the smaller rooms."

Marla gave a nod, for once glad to give in.

Jace laid down drop cloths while Marla arranged old sheets over the desks and opened windows to let in fresh air. Then the painting got underway. The weather turned hot and she was glad to be wearing khaki shorts and an old white tank top now dappled with paint splatters.

After a while, Marla swiped perspiration from her eyes. "Wish the air-conditioner worked," she said, a wistful note in her voice.

"One more thing that'll need fixing. Maybe we can get Blakely, the electrician, to donate his time."

"It won't hurt asking, though he's not exactly the philanthropic type," she said. "I can only imagine what it will be like if it isn't repaired once school starts."

"You'd have a lot of lethargic kids slumping at these desks. I'll put pressure on Blakely. I think a couple of his kids will be coming to school here."

"This fresh color transforms these walls as if by magic," she said, taking a moment to admire them. "Don't you think they look super?"

"Sure," he replied.

"I haven't had a paint brush in my hands since I painted billowing white clouds on my bedroom ceiling when I was a teenager."

"Clouds, huh," he said, and repositioned the ladder.

She glanced at the supple muscles working in Jace's arm as he raised the paintbrush to the room's ceiling and made even strokes. The sensuous movement caused her to pause in her own work.

"Those clouds help you sleep?" he asked with a grin when he caught her staring at him.

"I can't remember," she answered, and returned to her work.

Marla tried to keep her gaze from drifting back to Jace. Her arms soon ached. Rubbing her forearms, she leaned against the unpainted part of the wall and sighed. Jace was halfway across the ceiling.

"I hope you don't fall off that ladder," she teased.

Jace's back muscles rippled with a brawny grace, causing a tug deep inside her. This was no time to be thinking of personal things, she reminded herself.

"I don't intend to," he said, giving her an unhurried glance.

She cleared her throat. "I have to admit you're good."

He winked. "Well, I'd rather get a compliment any day than a complaint."

Watching Jace's sinewy arm pump strength into his big hand as he painted made her realize she was more than physically attracted to him. An unexpected thudding began in her chest.

Marla started to speak but found herself tongue-tied. He glanced down at her. "What?"

She swallowed hard. "I just want you to know I appreciate all the effort you're putting into this. You must have plenty of chores waiting for you back at the ranch."

"Hey, this is fun. Like taking a vacation."

Marla chuckled. "Yeah, sure. Still, I owe you one." She returned to painting, but couldn't help notice Jace watching her when his intense eyes swung to her hips. It rattled her. "C'mon," she said. "Get back to work."

Jace grinned. "I'm very proud of you, Marla," he said in a deep voice.

"Thanks," she blurted.

"I was just thinking how much Coyote Springs is indebted to you for taking this on. You've turned into a woman with a remarkable social conscience. The children can live like normal kids now and not spend half their lives on a bus."

Jace's remarks floored her, making her feel all mushy inside. "I don't know what to say, but you're giving me entirely too much praise." She felt like crying, and considered telling him all her shortcomings, so he wouldn't put her on one of those pedestals people talk about.

Jace's eyes warmed. *Why hadn't I realized how shockingly kind he was, how big hearted*? she asked herself.

Marla changed the subject before Jace could say something else to stir her up. "You'll make a fine coach," she said, visualizing him working with the boys like he did with his own nephew. The thought of his easy manner preceded another, that he'd make a terrific father, and it brought a smile to her lips.

"I like kids," he said.

"You *do* still plan to coach the boys, don't you?"

"Of course."

"Debra said you'd gotten an outstanding athletic award in college for basketball."

Jace looked at her with those intense eyes. "It wasn't much. Actually, I wanted to be a coach."

"Why didn't you pursue it?"

"Oh, things."

"Like what?"

"Like I had to drop out of the university and come home when Dad died."

Jace said it straight out, not feeling sorry for himself. He was the kind of man who did what needed to be done and she admired him for it. He finished the ceiling, then helped her complete her task.

Paint fumes caused Marla to sneeze as she stared at the smears on her arms and hands. A patch of paint on Jace's nose caused her to chuckle.

"What's so funny?" he asked.

"Your nose. You put me in mind of a clown."

"A clown!" He puffed up with feigned annoyance. "I've had gals tell me my Mel Gibson-esque nose is my best feature."

She giggled. "Not with that paint splotch on it."

He ran a finger over the white blob, spreading it, then dipped his index finger in the paint can, pulled it out, and swiped it across hers. "Now my beauty, we'll run off to the circus together."

"Darn you, Jace," she screeched as she pulled a tissue from her pocket and made an effort to remove the paint.

Having difficulty controlling his laughter, he said, "Let me."

"No thanks. I can do it myself." She started for the girls restroom. "And don't stop painting while I'm gone," she called over her shoulder.

"Slave driver," he muttered.

They worked all afternoon, taking time only to eat the cheese sandwiches she'd brought along. Marla stood back to admire their efforts. "This place is looking almost livable, thanks to you."

Jace shrugged off the praise and gave her a wry grin. "No problem," he said.

"I feel we've accomplished something here today."

"You should be proud," he said. "The place sure as heck doesn't look the same. It's gone from prison drab to bright sunlight, like your pretty face."

Marla turned to Jace, wanting so much to hug him, but contained the urge. She gave him a smile instead. "That about wraps it up for today."

"We'll need to tackle the outside next," he said. "I

could do it this weekend, and this time I'm bringing some of the boys from the ranch."

Marla agreed. "I'll come back tomorrow and scrub these desks," she said, suddenly so tired that every muscle in her body hurt.

"Uh, what time? I'll be here."

"I can't let you volunteer on this one. Really, I can take care of things."

Jace curled a corner of his mouth. "I'll be here, anyway."

"I'm grateful for all you've done," she said, gesturing at the super-clean walls. "School will open in a couple of weeks and the school board has already put the notice in the newspaper. Still, there's a lot to do."

"Call me anytime."

It pleased Marla that Jace wanted to be with her, and in truth she enjoyed having him around. She'd known him all her life but not in this new context. It was like getting to know someone all over again and seeing new facets to their personality.

"My 'to-do' list is a yard long but hopefully it'll all come together," Marla told him.

Jace glanced toward the playground and his eyebrows drew together. "With all those thorny weeds, I wouldn't put a billy goat out there. The basketball court needs repairing, too," he said. Then his eyes lit up. "Talked to the volunteer firemen. They agreed to come over tomorrow to clear the weeds."

"That's a relief," Marla said. "Something else I can check off my list."

"Like I said, a lot can get accomplished when a town pulls together."

They packed up everything. Jace gazed across the playground to the paint-chipped basketball backboard. "I can almost see the boys throwing baskets and making shots. Might have a real team yet."

"Why not?" Marla asked.

Jace was an intelligent man and she admired him more and more. As for a close, personal relationship, that seemed out of the question. Yet when he gave her that certain look, it caused her heart to flutter. However, the last "burn" had left her plenty wary of forming another alliance. Besides, once school opened she'd be too busy to think of anything else.

"What's gotta be done next, other than the desks?" he asked, breaking into her thoughts.

"Hmm," she said, glad to be distracted from those ticklish notions zooming around in her brain. "The boxes of supplies need to be stored and book covers cleaned."

Standing straight and tall in front of Marla, Jace smiled down at her with the very smile that could charm her down to her toes. "At your service, miss," he said. "But I don't think I ever heard of cleaning book covers."

Marla let loose with her own smile. "Now you know teachers have all sorts of boring jobs to do. Invisible leprechauns don't do these things for them."

Jace laughed. He could be exasperating, playful, hard-nosed, and focused, but also tender. It was the tender side she'd have to watch out for if she was going to keep her sense of balance in this relationship.

"It's good to have you home, Marla," he said, taking her hand, his voice a soft caress.

"Thanks. It's good to be home." She removed her hand. "Funny how things don't always work out the way people . . ." She started to say "want" but said "expect," instead.

His eyes darkened. "You're not tied here forever. In June, school will be out and you can go to work in the city, if that's what you want."

Marla considered his suggestion. "I've made my decision," she said. "And I'm not sorry for it. I have no plans to move away now."

Before she realized what he was about to do, he folded her into his arms and his warm lips brushed against hers. Her own parted eagerly. The kiss was as natural as breathing, except for the thrill racing through her body. Then he released her and stepped back. Unsteady on her feet, she took in a deep breath, completely forgetting everything but the marvelously brief encounter.

"Tomorrow, then," he said, as though trying to read her reaction.

"Tomorrow," she managed to get out, her knees as wobbly as a foal's.

Jace tipped his hat, slid into the cab of the truck, put it into gear, and drove away. Marla's fingertips tingled as she touched her lips. Then, gathering herself together, she plunged her hand in her purse and dug for her keys, thinking that all together, it had been a very productive day.

A sudden sound, no more than a whisper, caught Marla's attention. Alone, she glanced about. The building had already been locked. It must be the soft breeze worrying the cottonwood trees, she reasoned. Dismissing it, she climbed behind the Jeep's wheel, inserted the key, and heard the engine turn over.

Thoughts of Jace came racing back as she drove from

the parking lot. And oh, that gentle kiss! Being near him had caused her to feel so alive. She chuckled. He and his infectious optimism! Having him around was like being backed up by the cavalry. She snapped her fingers. Just like that, he'd become a dominant feature in her world.

Chapter Twelve

J ace drove back to the sprawling ranch, weary but exhilarated from being able to spend so much time with Marla, leaving him with a feeling of sweet intoxication. His arms were dotted with paint, putting him in mind of a leopard. Would he ever be the same? Marla! Marla! Marla! Even her name gave him pleasure, and he let a wide grin crisscross his rugged features.

Face it, he told himself, *you're head-over-boot-heels in love with the grown-up lady.*

He had a suspicion she thought he was the town lothario. Could he convince her of his sincerity? He'd never cared this much about a woman in his entire life, nor had he ever told anyone he loved them, for that matter. He'd held the words *I love you*, aloft as being something very special.

Jace had sensed Marla back away from him emotionally whenever he got too close, except for the kiss he'd given her. They'd briefly connected like a whirlwind.

132

Even so, it occurred to him she might be in love with someone else, someone she left behind in Flagstaff. The thought seared his gut like heartburn.

My Marla! Lately, in his mind, she'd become *his* Marla. Jace saw something remarkable in her, the way she was so determined to make a difference. He wanted to be with her, wanted her bad, and was more than willing to prove his love. But how could he show her they were meant for each other? And how could he get close when impediments kept jumping in the way like a bunch of jackrabbits?

Jace laid part of the problem at his own feet. Marla was now totally engrossed in opening the school, which after all, had been his brainchild. At least she was willing to let him be a part of the goings-on, which pleased him enormously. He was more than glad to do anything to help her make a success of the venture.

Jace thought about how Marla had readily taken on the immense job, and he knew she'd make it work one way or the other. His prime objective had been to keep her in the valley. If that was selfish of him, then so be it. He never said he was a saint.

Reaching the ranch, Jace unfolded his long legs from the truck and got out. Ripping his mind from the captivating Marla, he suddenly remembered he hadn't finished the work on the tractor, and jogged toward the barn.

The morning sun slanted through the trees along the road, making a mosaic, as Jace drove over to the Shelton ranch to see his neighbor Charlie. He found the older man sitting on a warped wooden bench not more than a stone's throw from the corral, his white cast thrust in front of him like a weapon.

"Hey," Charlie said with a smile and an outstretched hand when he saw Jace walking toward him. "What's up, neighbor?"

They exchanged a handshake. "How's it going?" Jace asked. "Thought I'd catch you having breakfast in bed. JoAnn said you were out here."

"Hate breakfast in bed. I ain't no lord of the manor," Charlie sneered.

Jace pushed back his hat. "Didn't expect to find you on the job so early."

Charlie shook his head. "You won't catch me sleeping in when there's work to do." He lowered his voice. "Wanted to come out here and see what Hull's been up to," he said in an annoyed voice. "Marla wanted to let him go but I had to countermand her. Gave him a good talking to, though."

That was news to Jace. Grant Hull glanced toward them, then looked away. The trainer was working with one of the yearlings without much success, by the looks of it. The young horse didn't want to obey the man's direction and Hull, face red with pent-up irritation, jerked the reins.

Jace didn't think much of the trainer and this only added to his disgust.

"Now, isn't he a piece of work," Charlie sputtered behind his raised hand. "But I gotta keep him on for awhile. We're shorthanded." The skin had webbed around the corners of Charlie's eyes and his mouth screwed up in frustration. "Deadlines! Marla's so dang busy with the school and all, she hardly has time to help with the chores. Still, I don't begrudge her taking it on, but it's not the best time in the world, as you very well know."

"Marla told me about a problem with Hull," Jace said, keeping his voice low-pitched.

"I'm surprised she said anything. You know how she is."

"I have a feeling she doesn't tell me a whole lot."

Charlie shrugged. Jace turned his back away from the trainer and pinned his gaze on his old friend. "Charlie, if Hull's a trainer with any reputation at all, my Aunt Josie owns Seabiscuit. Why, anyone can see the man doesn't know what he's doing."

The horse snorted and reeled backward as Hull cursed, yanking the reins in an attempt to control the animal. Jace wheeled on his heel and marched ram-rod straight to the fence separating them, something sour rising in his throat. He balled his fists and called tersely, "Don't jerk the reins like that, Hull. You got that yearling all strung out."

Hull glowered. "I'll take care of things, Van Garrett. Leave me be."

Jace wasn't to be put off. "Say, how long have you been working with cutting horses?"

Hull grimaced. "For more years than you can count up to," he said in a harsh voice. Shoulders squared like a boxer, the man reversed his baseball cap.

Jace shook his head wordlessly. He didn't want to get into a fight with the guy, though he was sorely tempted. As Charlie said, he needed him.

Charlie fretted on the bench and shifted his injured

leg. Jace walked back to him. Hull got the horse settled and led him away.

"Wish Marla had never hired the fool in the first place," Charlie muttered. "Shoulda' sent him packing right off and hired someone else. Now it's too late. Me being laid up has surely thrown a wrench in things around here."

"Couldn't be helped," Jace said.

"The doc won't hear of my getting inside the corral with the horses yet. Said another injury could make me a cripple for life."

"You listen to that doctor," Jace insisted. He wondered what he could do to help. However, his own time was stretched as thin as a lariat. Still, he asked. "What can I do?"

"We'll make it," Charlie said.

Things had taken an unexpected turn. Not in Marla's wildest imaginings had she believed she'd be given the opportunity to teach in her own community. In fact, she'd expected a Riverdance-like stomp of disapproval from the governing board when she'd made the proposal. Pride welled in her chest. She felt tingly. Bursting. Thrilled.

Although Jace helped her enormously, had even pushed her into this, it was Marla's own perseverance that made it happen. Now school was about to open and she rushed to town, making mental notes of all the things that needed to be done. This would not be a flick-of-the-wrist endeavor. No, it would take all her strength and resilience to pull it off.

Marla was giddy with excitement even while doubts

assailed her. She might be in way over her head. Sure, the building had been painted, the schoolyard cleared, colorful zinnias planted out front, the flag ready to hang on the pole, but that was only the outer part. A quiver ricocheted through her stomach as she parked in her slot. Stepping away from the Jeep, she gazed up at the old structure, barely able to suppress her high spirits.

"Yes! Yes! Yes!" she cried. "My baby!"

Of course she could do this. A smile skimmed across her face, warming her cheeks. She suddenly found herself in one of those moods where everything seems plausible and infinitely reasonable.

The children were already trooping into the yard. Things got underway with the Pledge of Allegiance. Morning activities whipped along with Marla so completely engrossed she forgot the time.

Jace came by during the lunch break when Marla had slipped into her office for a few minutes. Two volunteers were keeping their eyes on the children in the yard. "Bet you forgot to bring anything to eat," he said, holding up a sack. "I brought you a chicken burger. No fries."

"Thanks, Jace. Sounds great. I am feeling a bit hungry. This has been such a busy morning. I needed a dozen hands. Thank heavens for Debra and Judy. You just missed them."

He handed her the sack and took the chair across the desk from her. "You'll get everything under control in no time."

"I guess you could call this a work in progress, but I'm trying to make every moment count. There just doesn't seem to be enough moments."

He grinned. "You'll manage."

"Oh, Jace, sometimes I think the odds are stacked too heavily against me," she blurted, giving away a secret she'd kept tucked inside her.

"C'mon, sunshine," he said. "You'll figure out how to beat it, and I'll be here tomorrow afternoon to whisk the boys into shape. Hey, I can hardly wait. I always liked this coaching stuff."

"You have no idea how much I appreciate your volunteering. By the way, Debra's good with kids."

His eyes rested on hers. "I'm sure you are too."

That made Marla feel better. "I think I am. At least I try hard."

"Go on and eat your burger while it's hot." He picked up the sack she'd set on the desk, removed the chicken burger wrapper, and handed the fast food back to her.

Marla took a bite. "Tastes yummy," she said. "I was hungry and didn't know it."

Jace's smile was warm and reassuring, then his features grew serious. "You wouldn't mind if we started with basketball first, would you?"

Marla took only a moment to answer. "Sounds fine to me, since there are barely enough boys to play baseball. However, I'm wondering how you're going to handle their different ages and sizes?"

"That'll take some doing, won't it?"

She chuckled. "You've got your work cut out for you. My old friend Jean Roman said she'd work with the girls. She was quite an athlete in high school. To tell you the truth, I was envious of her. That's when there was a high school here, of course."

"They could have rebuilt it after the fire, but then the

Borax plant closed. The town shrank and the board of education wouldn't consider it."

"Yeah." She leaned back, stretching her sore muscles. "I can't believe this school is actually open."

"I know how much it means to you. I'm so proud of you for achieving your goal."

"I couldn't have done it without you," she said.

Jace reached across the desk and wiped a corner of her mouth where a dab of barbecue sauce had lodged. "Gosh, but you're gorgeous, sauce and all."

His eyes flashed over her face and settled on her lower lip. Marla felt the warm connection with him and braced herself for the kiss that was sure to follow. But he didn't try to kiss her. Flustered by her own desire, she took a much needed breath. "It's time for me to relieve the others," she said, and stood up, dusting crumbs from her denim skirt.

"You didn't finish your burger."

"Oh." Not wanting to disappoint him, Marla took her seat and finished it, washing it down with cold coffee.

Outside, a babble of voices sounded like a bunch of angry chickens. Marla and Jace left the office and joined the volunteer, Mrs. Varnell, who was attempting to quell a fight between two boys.

Jace spread his hands and pulled a face. "What's going on?" he demanded in a stern voice.

The boys quickly ceased their combat. "He said my sandwich was no good," one of the boys said. His hair was dark, his eyes a rich brown.

"Is that right?" Jace said. "What kind is it?"

"Burrito."

"Why, that's one of my favorites. You're mighty

lucky." He gazed at the other boy, who's anger changed to chagrin. "You got a problem with his sandwich?"

"I guess not," the boy muttered.

"Good. Okay, you can go eat your own lunch. Like now."

"I'm sorry," the boy said to his schoolmate.

The matter settled, the boys walked away in opposite directions. Jace turned to Marla and Mrs. Varnell. "Kids."

"You handled that well," Marla said. "Thanks again for the burger."

Jace smiled and tipped his broad-brimmed hat to the women. Marla watched him saunter away, his shoulders straight, and thought how nice it was to be seeing more of him.

The clock chimed the midnight hour. Marla worked at her desk at home on lesson plans until her eyes grew bleary, then tottered upstairs to bed. Moonlight glazed across the bedspread. She switched on the light and crossed the room to the window to close the blinds. The sound of a frog broke the silence outside.

Marla dumped her clothes on the straight-backed chair, slipped a nightgown over her head, then drew back the bedspread. She stared at the muted shadows on the ceiling as she laid there, her mind unwilling to release its energy and let her sleep. After awhile an odd sensation came over her—as though someone beyond the window was watching her.

Marla told herself to quit being a silly goose and pulled the sheet over her head. Yet it occurred to her the house might have ghosts. Maybe her favorite grandmother. But that was an even sillier notion. She understood very well that the mind could play tricks on people at night, especially when they were having a bout of sleeplessness. Finally, she told herself she didn't care if she slept or not and almost immediately dozed off.

Marla dreamed about Jace. They were back on the trail with the mules. He prevented one of the more surly ones from stomping her when she fell, and carried her away from danger in his strong arms. Clearly, the man had become a big part of the fabric of her life, even in her dreams.

The first week of school ended on a reasonably successful note, though at times Marla felt like one of those little caged hamsters on a wheel. The children's sunny faces had become more familiar. Her volunteer helpers continued to be enthusiastic. Jace showed the boys how to do drills and handle a basketball. One of them, twelve-year-old Jimmy Henderson, showed an aptitude for sports. Angela Jones, nine, helped Marla after school, the little girl eager to help. All the children had their strengths and weaknesses, and Marla was learning how to deal with them.

Jace hadn't finished his after school coaching session, though he was about ready to wrap things up when Marla joined him. She admired the patient way he handled children and taught the boys about teamwork.

"The younger ones are surprisingly good at dribbling the ball," Jace told her. Marla could tell by his demeanor that he liked this activity. With quiet authority, he was building their trust, as well.

"So you've thrown yourself into yet another responsibility, ranching and being the town fire chief not enough for you," she teased, then tapped her watch. "Time to pack it in, coach."

Jace grinned, scarcely taking his eyes from the boys as they eagerly bounded up and down the court, honing their ball passing abilities and blocking shots.

"Ten minutes and we're out'a here," Jace said.

Marla walked back to her office. Like clock work, Jace came through the office door, sweat on his brow, his hair mussed. "You still here?"

"I'm always the last to leave, remember?" Marla said, putting aside a form she'd been working on. "Hey, you were great out there."

Jace's eyes brightened. "Thanks. Working with the boys showed me how out of condition I am." He rubbed his back as though in pain and laughed.

"I don't believe that for a minute," she said with a grin.

Jace held up his upper arm and flexed his considerable muscle. "Want to see how weak this is? Give me your hand."

She pursed her lips and held back. "I definitely do not."

He chuckled, then lowered his arm.

Marla gave him a reflective look. "The early years of a child's life are so impressionable," she said. "Jimmy Henderson ought to do just fine, yet I can't help worrying about Angela Jones."

"Yeah," Jace agreed. "I heard about her mother up and leaving. Darn shame."

"I only hope the woman decides to come home soon."

Jace smiled. "Seems like you're learning there's more to teaching than, uh, teaching," he said.

"You're so right about that."

"By the way, why don't we drive over to Flagstaff tomorrow and take in a movie?"

"I haven't been to a flick in ages," she said, perking up. "Tell you what, you can persuade me if you pick a comedy, but it will have to be the following weekend. I'm too busy right now." Then she sighed. Why did she always have to be in control, even to what movie they'd see? Clearing her throat, she added, "I don't care which one we go to. You pick it."

He gave her a big grin. "Cool. Next weekend then."

Pleased with Jace's enthusiasm, it again occurred to Marla he'd make a wonderful father, but she quickly set that thought on a back burner.

On Saturday morning Marla finished stocking the library shelves with new books before standing back to admire her work. Like a fruit picker, she'd handpicked each book in order to give the students the best advantage. She thought about Jace and how he took an interest in everything she did. Without his support she'd never have been able to pull all this together. Could she ever thank him enough?

Marla threw away the empty book boxes. When she came back, someone tapped on the door. Jace stood framed there. Her heart skipped a beat and she smiled. "You scared me," she said. "I wasn't expecting anyone."

"Sorry, hon," Jace said as he sauntered across the floor.

Marla went back to tidying the place. Jace came up

behind her and reached his face around to nuzzle her temple, his arms encircling her waist. "Still like teaching?" he murmured.

An electrifying shiver ran through her body, so strong she could scarcely answer him. "I'm too tired to tell," she managed to say, trying to hide her feelings.

"Poor baby," he cooed.

Reluctantly, Marla stepped away from his embrace. In a flash, he drew her back to him. She didn't make even the slightest move to resist this time. He tipped her chin with his thumb and smothered her lips with his own, overwhelming her with giddy desire.

"Darling," he murmured in her ear, "I want you so much."

Her body tingled, and she wanted him. "Oh, Jace . . ."

Kissing his intoxicating lips was exactly what Marla had told herself she shouldn't be doing, yet how could she do otherwise when he was holding her so close?

However, their heightened moment of passion waned and Marla found the courage to free herself from his embrace and catch her breath. "You certainly know how to make a gal forget everything but you," she said with a demi-grin. "Now get out'a here and let me finish my work."

Jace turned off the shower and stepped onto the bathroom rug, water running in tiny rivulets down his body as he toweled off. He felt good. More than good. He was taking Marla to Flagstaff, their first real date, and he wanted it to go well. He dressed with more care than usual, shaved carefully, then combed his dark hair into place.

By the time he left the house, late afternoon shadows crept below the mountain range. He thought about how Marla had let him kiss her and found himself humming. Marla was some gal. He admired her tenacity and how she kept on going in the face of all she had to do. Teaching classes, acting as principal and helping to run the ranch, had to be a gigantic load. Jace thought about Hull. So the Shelton's had had problems with him. When Jace found time, he'd telephone some people he knew in Florida, see what he could find out about the guy.

Jace started the truck's engine. His mood lightened as he backed up, headed down the washboard road, and crossed the cattle guard. Beyond, the darkening hillside was sprinkled with oak and pinon. Seeing it always brought on a peaceful feeling, but not this time. He was too excited at the prospect of seeing Marla.

He turned onto the main road and headed east. The entrance to the Shelton ranch loomed ahead and he flipped on his turn signal, then drove between the wrought-iron gates. He faced the unmitigated fact that he'd fallen in love with Marla, and could no longer call it infatuation. If he read her right, Marla was also attracted to him. Yet he didn't know whether she shared his deeper feelings—those of love.

Jace thought about it as he pulled up in the yard beside the two-story ranch house. So often when he tried to get close to Marla, she'd get all involved with other matters. However, she hadn't been too busy for his kisses. A sudden glow warmed his insides, just thinking about how good it felt to have her in his arms.

One part of him almost wished she hadn't opened the school, since it consumed a great big bundle of her time.

On the other hand, it kept her from moving away, didn't it? These thoughts made him feel a tad guilty, but not for long.

Jace switched off the engine and glanced up at the house. Marla was so different from other women. He knew she kept things in when he wanted her to share her thoughts with him, and she could be real controlling, but it didn't bother him much. It suddenly occurred to him she might not trust him, a thought he didn't want to dwell on.

Jace got out and stretched his legs. He'd been up since before dawn herding cattle, playing catch-up as usual, before heading over to the school to help Marla. All day he'd thought about their date, what they'd talk about. Would he bore her?

Marla was standing on the front porch. The overhead porch fixture illuminated her shiny hair and her brilliant smile. "Right on time," she said.

Jace beamed. "Yeah. Let's get going."

They headed toward Flagstaff fifty miles away. Having Marla in the truck beside him was like heaven and he hardly heard the thrum of the engine as a wave of tenderness engulfed him. He caught the scent of her flowery cologne and it did things to his male hormones, though he didn't let on.

"I've been looking forward to this," she said, settling herself.

He gave her a sidelong glance. "Me too."

She glanced away and gazed through the window at the darkening landscape. "Autumn will be here before we know it," she said. "Last night was a little on the nippy side." She pulled her jacket closer to her.

"You look great in that blue dress," he said.

She turned back to him. "It's lavender, but thanks."

He wondered if she was nervous. "I thought we'd get a bite to eat before the show starts."

"Fine," she said.

They reached the outskirts of town. Jace pulled off the freeway and drove into a restaurant parking slot across the street from an RV campground surrounded by fragrant pine trees. He thought about telling Marla he'd gotten back a report from the cutting horse association on Hull, but changed his mind. It was favorable. Still, Jace planned to make a couple of calls when he got around to it. Something just didn't seem right.

He opened the truck door for Marla and she slid out, straight into his arms. The close contact made him want to plant a sizzling kiss on her lips but he let her go instead. He'd promised to keep his hands to himself, yet dog-gone, it was going to prove a much harder task than roping a steer.

Jace gave a chuckle and escorted Marla into the restaurant. A hostess led them to a table by a giant river-rock fireplace. Marla seemed delighted by the romantic atmosphere of oak, paintings, and flowers.

Jace ordered steak and Marla ordered salmon. They sat near a fireplace enjoying their drinks. She rested her hand on the table and he reached across to wrap it gently in his own.

"This is nice," Marla said. "I've never been here, even though I attended Northern Arizona University. It was mostly all work and no play."

"I went to Albuquerque until I dropped out. But that's an old story."

"You wanted to coach, didn't you? Ever consider going back?"

"Not anymore. Besides, I'm finally a full-fledged coach, thanks to you." He gave her a wide grin. "And now I'm sitting here with the girl of my dreams. That's real special."

"What a lovely thing to say, Jace. Thanks. I feel the same way."

Marla searched his face and saw Jace's eyes soften as his lips parted.

"You know I care about you, don't you, hon?" he said.

Marla felt goose-bumps on her arms. "Yes," she admitted, but something made her hold her tongue about her own feelings toward him and she didn't go on.

Jace's handsome face creased, making him even more handsome. "You also know you're the prettiest gal in this room tonight, don't you?"

"Oh, Jace. I do believe you've gone blind," she countered, then remembered that his mother was blind and hoped he didn't take offense.

He hadn't. Throwing back his head, he laughed. The waiter appeared with the salads they'd ordered and they turned their attention to eating. Marla could tell by Jace's features he was enjoying himself as he attacked the pile of greens and tomato wedges in the bowl.

Halfway through the meal the tinkling sounds of a piano caused Marla to glance across the floor. All of a sudden floodlights flickered on a stage she hadn't noticed. Singers, some of them she recognized as waiters, ambled onto the stage dressed in western costumes, their voices raised in a song from *Annie Get Your Gun*.

"I didn't know this place had live entertainment," Marla said, excited.

"You said you wanted to see a show that was funny. Well, here it is."

"What a fantastic surprise," she exclaimed.

Instantly caught up in the show, Marla thumped her foot under the table to the beat of the music. She hadn't laughed so much in ages.

Then the grand finale arrived to much clapping by the audience, followed by an encore. The lights dimmed and the stage returned to oblivion again.

"Did you enjoy it?" Jace asked. A smile worked across the breadth of his face.

"I loved it!" Marla reached across the table and touched the back of his hand. "So this was the show you were going to take me to? Well, I adored every minute of it."

"That's what I wanted," Jace said. "You needed a night out to relax, have a good time."

"You certainly amaze me. I would never have guessed."

He looked pleased.

"Then you've been here before?" she asked.

His eyes glittered. "Not for a long time."

Marla wondered if Jace had brought some other woman he'd cared about. The thought gave her a jealous moment and she smiled at her own folly.

After all, she and Jace were only good friends. Well, maybe a little more than that, if she were honest.

The three-quarter moon had reached it's waning position when Jace brought Marla back to the Shelton ranch. No lights shown in the old house. She felt a little guilty because she'd had so little time to visit with her father, but she wasn't sorry she'd gone out with Jace.

He walked her to the door and took her hand, then gently played with her fingers. "I had a real good time," he said.

"Me too," she replied. "I can't remember when I enjoyed anything so much. I've always loved music."

Jace kissed the tip of her index finger, following it one by one. "Then we'll have to do it again real soon," he said, his voice low and caressing.

"I'd like that," Marla said with emotion. A silence fell between them as Jace held her hand, his eyes devouring her in the faint light from the stars. Marla took a step closer to him. She knew he wanted to kiss her and she waited anxiously, nerves jangling together like an unstrung guitar. Then it happened and she savored the taste of him, the feel of his lips covering hers, the warmth of his skin.

"Darling," he said, his tone husky. "I'm crazy about you. You must know that."

Marla felt as though she'd been transported to heaven and back. Her limbs were like putty and she could barely speak above a whisper. "I know, Jace."

He drew her closer into a loving embrace and kissed her until she felt dizzy. Breathless, she backed away and giggled, surprising herself. "I've got to go in," she said. "It's late."

"Must you?" His voice flooded with emotion.

She wanted desperately to stay with him. "I've got to get up at dawn. You probably do too. Thanks for a lovely evening. I had such a good time." Then she turned away, opened the door, and called over her shoulder, "Night, now, cowboy."

"Yeah," he said, his voice rich with meaning. "See you around."

She closed the door softly behind her. Sinking against it, she hugged herself. What a grand night! The sound of the pickup truck's engine brought her around and she peeked out the window in time to see its taillights recede down the driveway. For a moment she wanted him to come back. His kisses had been more than just kisses, they had ignited her longing to experience every part of him.

The week zipped by in a flash, then it was Friday again. In the classroom, Marla's throat felt like she'd swallowed chalk dust. Could she do this day after day? But of course she could. Tomorrow, she'd catch an early flight from Flagstaff to Las Vegas in order to see Jace compete in the national rodeo competition. He'd already gone ahead with his two best roping horses, telling her he planned to have a good time no matter whether he won or lost. All the same, Marla, aware of his competitive nature, knew he'd give it his best shot.

Marla planned to share a room at the Golden Nugget Hotel in downtown Las Vegas with Debra and Mary Van Garrett. She'd never been to the glitzy city and looked forward to the weekend. However, in the back of her mind, she worried about Jace. Those bulls had to be even more treacherous than the animal he'd ridden in Coyote Springs. She prayed he wouldn't break his neck.

* * *

Marla's flight was temporarily delayed, causing her to be a half hour late. The Golden Nugget Hotel was smaller than some of the posh new ones like the Bellagio. Debra and her mother were already downstairs waiting for a shuttle to take them to the arena when Marla located them.

"I'll run my suitcase upstairs and join you right away," Marla said after they greeted each other with warm hugs.

Debra gave her a card key. "You better hurry," she said. "The shuttle should be here pretty soon."

Marla did as her friend directed and found the room they'd be sharing. Halfway back to the elevator, she realized that in her haste she'd accidentally locked her purse in the room. Key, arena ticket, everything was in the purse. Feeling every inch an idiot, she found a house phone, frantically called the concierge and explained what had happened. In a matter of minutes, a man with a hotel badge on his lapel arrived to assist her. However, before he would unlock the door, he gave her quite a grilling about her identity.

Stressed, Marla could almost see the three women missing the opening ceremonies of the rodeo because of her stupidity. Finally, she had her purse in hand, thanked the man for his help, and took the elevator down to the main floor.

They reached the stadium in time and found seats. Five minutes later, horses with colorful banners began to parade around the vast arena. A roar traveled through the crowd as things cleared and the calf roping event got underway.

"I may not be able to see what's going on," Mary said,

"but I can hear all the excitement. It's wonderful. Debra, you'll tell me when Jace is up, won't you?"

"Of course I will, Mom," Debra said.

It was obvious Mary wanted to be there in case anything happened to her son—good or bad. Dressed in a turquoise pantsuit, she looked just the right shade of a Western lady, Las Vegas style. A smart white cowgirl hat trimmed with peacock-blue feathers sat atop her dark hair.

One by one riders shot out of the gate zeroing in on reluctant calves like Kamikaze pilots. The men lassoed the calves and brought them down with a thud in the loose dirt, before quickly tying their legs. So far the times weren't that outstanding. Would Jace do better?

Excitement spilled among the crowd as a well known country and western singer belted out a song. Then it was Jace Van Garrett's turn to hit the saddle. He mounted Gun Powder, a number nine pasted to the back of his plaid Western shirt. Chaps and a protective vest made up his safety gear.

Like a little girl, Marla crossed her fingers for luck. Then the gate swung open. Jace and his horse dove for the fast-moving calf. He hurled his lariat over his head with expert precision. Marla held her breath as the rope zipped right as the calf executed a sudden left, and the rope fell to the ground like a dead snake.

"What happened?" Mary demanded.

"Jace blew it," Debra told her mother. "The calf's running merrily off, practically thumbing its nose at him."

"Oh, my," Mary said, clutching her purse.

Marla knew how disappointed Jace must be as the crowd heaved a disappointed sigh that rippled through the grandstands. "Can't win 'em all," she said in order to make Mary feel better.

"Let's see what happens next," Mary said, putting on a good face.

The bucking bronco event followed. Jace was the third rider called. Marla hoped he would do better this time. He hovered over the chute before dropping onto the saddle at the exact moment the gate sprang open.

Deadly Deed, the bay stallion, knew plenty of tricks. The horse bucked and kicked and reared, followed by devilish leaps and a breathtaking spin, its tail whipping like a medieval weapon. Twice Jace almost lost his balance but held on for the eight seconds before a relief rider rescued him. Marla and Debra jumped to their feet and cheered with enthusiasm.

Jace won the event and received a trophy. Elated, Marla called, "Way cool, Jace!"

Mary hugged both young women. "I knew he could do it," she said, slightly shaken.

The afternoon whizzed by. The women ate hot dogs and drank soft drinks. Marla spilled mustard on her black denim jeans but was too excited to care much. She wore a black Western-style shirt, her best boots, and a white hat with a snakeskin band, catching the eye of more than a few cowboys. One asked to take her to dinner after the rodeo. She politely declined, but it gave her a lift anyway.

The big bull riding competition came last. The announcer sounded like he'd just arrived from deep in the heart of the Texas panhandle. Marla's heart did a loop when she thought of Jace on the back of one of those mean brutes. Before he'd left, she had encouraged him to pass up this event, but he wouldn't listen.

Some of the riders looked like teenagers out for a thrill. One after another, they landed flat on their backs or bottoms or stomachs, the angry bulls having hammered and grilled them with bone-jarring leaps. Some riders limped from the field under their own steam while others had to be carried away on stretchers.

Jace's number came next. Marla sat frozen in her seat and said a quick prayer for his safety. The chute creaked open and the big bull charged into the arena with Jace on its back, his hat pulled low over his forehead. The monstrous animal kicked up dirt like a hailstorm. Jace's head jerked this way and that. Enormous bursts of energy whipped the bull into a frenzy as it sought to dislodge its rider, but Jace held on.

Then the buzzer sounded. Just as Jace leaped off the bull's back, it lunged to the side. Jace managed to land on his feet, though the bull was right behind him. One of the clowns steered it away with a flashing, bright orange flag. Jace jogged across the arena, a wide smile on his handsome face.

Marla knew he was in his element. More thrills and spills followed. However, another rider beat Jace's time by a mere second, leaving Jace to come in second. Marla was devastated. He had tried so hard, having taken his life in his hands.

Afterward, Jace met with the women and reassured them that he didn't mind losing. "There's always another opportunity," he said. "Heck, I'll make it yet."

"Now don't you be thinking of repeating this," his

mother cautioned. "You're getting too old for such hell raising."

He laughed, but Marla and Debra agreed with her.

They gathered together to dine at the Red Square at Mandalay Bay Resort and Casino before going on to the Flamingo to see the legendary Gladys Knight. Marla saw a different Mary. Animated and fun-loving, she teased her son then got caught up in the music. Marla wondered if Mary's lighthearted attitude was due to her relief that Jace didn't get hurt.

Afterward, they took a taxi back to the hotel. Jace insisted they have a cup of coffee with him before calling it a night. Mary and Debra bowed out, retiring gracefully. Alone, Marla and Jace wandered over to a quiet lounge and sat side by side on a sofa. A waitress took their orders.

"I haven't been alone with you all evening," Jace said, his brows meeting.

"Surely you didn't want your mom and Debra to eat dinner alone."

He blanched. "Of course not. I just wanted to have a little time alone with you."

She gave him a smile. "Well, here we are, big guy."

"Yeah. It's great." He wrapped her hand in his and held it, an act that had become very familiar of late.

Slot machines clacked noisily in the casino nearby but Marla ignored them. Being alone with Jace meant a lot to her, too.

"I'm going to teach you to gamble before we go upstairs," he said with a good-natured grin. "You might go home a winner."

"You mean there's a possibility that I might go from teacher to lady gambler?"

His eyes twinkled. "I won't hold my breath."

They finished their drinks and Jace paid the bill, then they sauntered into the casino. "You just insert your quarters in one of these machines and watch them be gobbled up," he said with a dry laugh. "That's about how it goes."

"Oh, c'mon. Some people must be winning or else they wouldn't come here."

"Want to bet on it?" he said, amused. "You saw all those great looking buildings today, didn't you? Guess who's money financed them. Tourists like us, that's who."

"Then why do you want me to try?"

"Never can tell," he said, his eyes rounding. "You might be blessed with Lady Luck."

"Now that you've got me all revved up, I have to at least try," she said with a grin.

"Go ahead." He handed her some coins.

Marla inserted a quarter and received five back. "It's easy," she said, teasing him. "I'll probably hit a jackpot with the next try."

"I wish you luck."

In the next few minutes Marla accumulated ten dollars, but soon lost it all. "So much for that," she said as they walked away arm in arm.

"Fate," he said.

Marla nodded. "It puts me in mind of that mean bull you rode today. You were lucky he didn't dump you on your ear."

Jace snickered. "That ol' bull wasn't so bad."

"I'm proud of you, all the same," Marla said.

He beamed. "I like to hear you say that."

"But promise me you won't ride anymore bulls, Jace," she asked, her voice taking on a serious note.

He scratched his jaw. "What are you willing to give up if I do?"

Marla hadn't expected that question. "I don't know. I'll have to think about it." Then she shocked herself by almost saying, "I'll marry you if you'll give up bull riding."

What was she thinking? Jace hadn't even suggested anything remotely like marriage. Wanting to wiggle out of anymore ticklish questions, she said, "It's time for bed. I don't want to wake your mom or Debra when I go upstairs."

Jace escorted Marla to the elevators and encircled her waist when they found themselves alone. She gazed up at him. "This weekend has been fun," she murmured.

"Sharing a part of it with you has been the best." He touched her cheek. "I'll pick you up in front of the hotel at a quarter after nine and drive you over to the airport tomorrow." He brightened. "Unless you want to ride back home with me."

"I can't," she said.

"Wish we could at least have breakfast but I've got to get the horses taken care of. Thanks for coming to the rodeo."

"I came to see you," she said softly.

"That takes an even bigger thanks, hon."

They got off the elevator and sauntered hand in hand down the corridor. When they reached Marla's room, she leaned against the door. Jace put both of his hands out to capture hers.

"You look so pretty tonight," he said. A corner of his mouth turned up in an irresistible smile.

"Thanks. You look pretty good, yourself. None of those men today compared with you."

That made him swell with pride. "Think so?"

"I know so."

"In what way?"

"Why, your expertise."

Jace's nearness played havoc with Marla's good senses. In order to escape her own urges, she freed her hands and fished in her purse for the plastic key.

"Not yet," Jace said, and his eyes danced. "Don't you think this day warrants a goodnight kiss?"

"Oh, why?" she asked in mock seriousness as he placed both hands on the wall, imprisoning her.

"Because you said I stood heads above all those other riders, that I was out and out virile, the most handsome, the most . . . uh . . ."

"I did not," she broke in with a chuckle. "You're exaggerating things here, buddy."

Jace laughed and drew Marla to him, then planted a hot kiss on her parted lips that almost caused her knees to buckle. The door opened behind her and she would have fallen inside if he hadn't been holding her. She and Jace stepped away from each other like high school kids caught necking on the front porch. Debra stood framed in the light.

"I thought I heard you out here," she said, unable to hide the grin on her face. She looked at first one then the other when neither of them spoke. "Uh, yes . . ." and closed the door.

Marla turned to Jace. "I better go in."

"Yeah."

"Goodnight."

Jace gave her a hurried hug then watched her go inside.

The day after Marla returned, she went looking for Grant Hull. She'd had a long talk with her father, who told her the trainer disappeared when she left to go to Las Vegas and had only just come back. Charlie was plenty ticked-off.

"Hull musta' been on a toot. Came back green around the gills," Charlie had said. "And Jeff caught him red-handed in town selling feed from the back of his truck to some rancher, shortchanging our livestock at a bad time like this."

It was an unforgivable act, and Marla was about to fire him once and for all. She found Hull sitting by the barn, leaning back in a chair, a piece of hay stuck between his teeth. She wondered if he was using it for chlorophyll, but the thought didn't amuse her one wit.

"Hull!" she shouted, walking up to him, her shoulders back, hoping the shock effect would give her the upper hand. "You've had it, mister. Get your things together and clear out."

He shot up, face puffy, eyes bleary. "You can't get rid of me that easy, little lady. Your dad said I could stay on. You forget that?"

"Dad and I are in complete agreement this time." Then she told Hull what she'd learned.

Hull looked defiant, not ready to give in. "I got a contract says I can work until the yearlings are shipped."

That was news to Marla. "I never gave you a contract," she said.

His chin jutted out. "Your dad did."

"Then show me."

This stumped him, and he couldn't produce the document. "You haven't bested me yet," he said, but she knew she had.

Marla watched the trainer walk away, his head hanging low on his chest.

Marla thought about her encounter with Hull through the prism of recent events as she waited for Jace to pick her up. He was taking her to Molly's for dinner. She hadn't seen that much of him, other than at school, since they'd gotten back from Las Vegas. They'd both been very busy.

Her father added to her worries, creating problems, too. Instead of helping, he sometimes got in the way in his attempt to get back in control of things. She couldn't allow him to work hands-on with the horses for fear they might accidentally bang against him and reinjure his leg.

Jace arrived at the ranch, his face creased with a smile as he helped Marla into the truck, but the smile soon changed to a frown of concern. "You look bushed," he said. "What's up?"

Though Marla hadn't intended to, she blurted, "I fired Hull."

"Finally. Well I'll be."

Then she told him what had happened and a murderous look came into his eyes. "It's over now and he's left the ranch, Jace. Let it go," she said.

"The darn idiot. He had a good job. But people like him don't know a good deal when they see it."

"We'll manage somehow without a trainer," she said. "Jeff has learned a lot and he'll fill in."

"I'll send over one of my guys too."

"Thanks." She felt better.

"What else?"

Marla swallowed. He could read her so easily. "Dad's trying to exert his independence. It's like a little power struggle going on all the time with him. And he's not well yet. The doctor said older people take longer to heal, but try and tell him that. He's so bullheaded."

Jace thought about what Marla said. "Why don't you two sit down and hash things out."

She gnawed the side of her lower lip. "I've tried, but you know Dad."

"Charlie's anxious to get back in the swing of things. You can understand that."

"Do you think I'm being too controlling?" she asked, though she didn't necessarily want to hear the answer.

Jace grinned. "You're a lot like Charlie. Before he got laid up, whenever he saw a problem, he'd set about solving it on the spot, but everything's changed. That's bound to bite at him."

Marla sighed. "He's always been so strong."

"Under normal circumstances, it makes for a darn good rancher." Jace took a quiet moment before adding, "Give yourself a break. You're working too hard."

"Mom says work has its peaks and troughs and things will level off, but I'd like to know when."

"The teaching part going okay?"

"I can't complain."

"I'm amazed at the energy you devote to the school."

"I do love my work and dearly want this to be a good year for the kids."

"Stop worrying. It'll be just fine."

Marla took a deep breath as the pickup truck headed toward town. "On a happier note, Angela's mother came home. I guess she has bouts of depression and goes away to stay with her sister when things get too heavy. Makes my heart feel good to see the child happy."

"Makes me feel good too," Jace said.

Marla heard the empathy in his voice. Jace Van Garrett had a tender side a mile long.

Molly's Coffee Shoppe loomed ahead. Jace turned on the directional light and pulled into the gravel parking lot. They got out and strolled inside, the noise level assailing Marla's ears.

"Did everyone in the valley decide to come here tonight at the same time?" she asked in wonder.

The lights flickered and everyone shouted, "Happy Birthday, Marla," and sang the traditional Happy Birthday song with gusto.

Shocked speechless, Marla stood stark still.

"Happy Birthday," Jace whispered in her ear, then gave her a little hug.

She turned to him, mouth open. "Why Jace Van Garrett, you never told me about this."

Everyone laughed and cheered as her cheeks flushed. Marla spotted her father and mother across the room sitting at a round table with Mary, Debra, her son, and husband.

Judy parted the crowd and gave Marla a big hug. "Well, say something, girlfriend. We're all here to celebrate your birthday."

Marla laughed. "Thanks for coming, everyone. This is such a special surprise."

Then some of the school children and their parents sang a school song Marla had taught them. She forced back tears. "This is wonderful," she said. "Thank you all."

The mayor stepped forward. "We're the ones who ought to thank you for keeping the school open, and we're here tonight to honor you."

Marla stammered, "Really, I can't believe this. No one hinted at anything."

Judy rolled out a tiered cake that looked more like a wedding cake than a birthday confection. Marla walked into the circle of friends and everyone talked at once as they patted her arm or gave her hugs and air kisses. Yellow and pink streamers and colored balloons added to the festivities.

Jace led her to the mayor's table where the school board members were gathered and took the seat beside her. A mariachi band threaded through the tables singing romantic songs.

"Having a good time, hon?" Jace asked.

"This is like some wondrous dream," she answered, and squeezed his hand under the table. "I'd practically forgotten it was my birthday."

Fried chicken, scalloped potatoes, creamed corn and hot biscuits, Molly's most popular menu items, were served. Miniature turkey candles decorated the tables, along with green tablecloths, something never before seen at Molly's. In the corner, stacks of colorfully wrapped gift boxes were on display.

JoAnn came over and kissed her daughter's cheek. "We're all so proud of you, sweetie," she said, her eyes moist.

"Oh, Mom," Marla said, and raised her arms to hug her mother. "You never even said a word about this."

JoAnn giggled. "You're not the only one who keeps secrets."

Later, tables were pushed back, the lights dimmed, and dancing began as the mariachis played.

Jace asked Marla to dance. She rose and glided into his arms as though she'd always been there. "I don't remember when I've been so happy," she said.

"You deserve it, hon. I told you the town was behind you all the way."

"This makes everything worth it, and then some."

His eyes devoured her. "That's good, darling."

"Darling." She rolled the word deliciously around on her tongue. "I like to hear you call me that."

Jace swung her around. She laughed, then glanced over his shoulder and saw her mother talking to Mary. JoAnn looked animated. Funny how parents got such enjoyment from their kids' small gains in life, Marla thought. It made her feel even better.

"We ought to circulate," Marla said when the music stopped.

Jace didn't look as though he totally agreed. "I'd rather keep you here in my arms," he said.

Her lips curled into a smile. "I wouldn't mind that myself, but we can't."

Marla started to walk on but Jace stopped her. "One moment, hon. I have a present for you too."

"Oh?"

He took a small box from his pocket and handed it to her. Marla recognized it immediately—a ring box—and her heart leaped. They stood in the middle of the floor as she untied the pearl white ribbon, opened the box, and gasped. A diamond engagement ring! Happiness surged through her like nothing she'd ever experienced.

"Well, will you?" Jace asked, his voice husky with emotion.

Marla threw her arms around his neck and kissed him, right there in front of everyone. "Oh, yes!" she cried.

The crowd clapped. "Leave it to you, Jace, to make your proposal a community affair," someone called as a cacophony of roars followed.

Marla was completely exhilarated. She laid her face against his shoulder.

When Marla came home from school early to get a report she'd left behind, she heard her father's angry voice coming from the stables, then another's. Hull? What was he doing here? She left the Jeep door ajar and hurried across the stableyard. Voices ratcheted upward, sounding as though the men were about to come to blows.

Marla's father was in no condition to be battling even a baby calf, let alone a big man like Hull. She opened the tack room door and saw the trainer leaning over the desk with the front of Charlie's shirt collar scruffed up in his big fist, the color draining from her father's face. Her heart lurched.

"You ornery old cuss," Hull spit in her father's face. "You owe me a thousand dollars back pay and I ain't leaving til I get it."

"Let go of me before I slap you down, you skunk!" Charlie croaked.

Marla slammed the door purposefully to get their attention, fearing the former trainer might throttle her father, if things didn't cool off. "What's going on?" she demanded.

Both men turned wide eyes to her and Hull released Charlie. Her father coughed and ran his palm over his throat. "This turkey says we owe him a thousand bucks, and when I said he's a bald-faced liar, he demanded Major if we don't pay. I wouldn't give even one of them mules to this scumbag."

Hull's face took on a brutal expression and he huffed, "Why I . . ." and drew back his fist.

Marla cut in sharply. "You know we paid you fair and square, Hull. As for Major, he's not going anywhere. Now that ought to settle things."

Charlie stood up on his legs, favoring the one in the cast. "Now clear out," he told Hull in a savage voice. "I don't want to ever see you around here again."

Hull pulled his hat low over his forehead. "You haven't heard the last of this," he shot back. "I intend to report you to the trainer's association. This place is a mess. You'll never get another trainer to set foot around here when I'm through."

Charlie turned livid and his eyes bulged. Marla was afraid he'd have a stroke. "Leave now," she told Hull. "This has gone on far enough."

The man didn't move. "It beats all," he said in a churlish tone. "After all I done for you folks."

Then he marched to the door and gave it a swift kick. The door slammed against the wall, shaking the building. But at least he had gone. Marla sighed with relief, glad she'd intervened before someone got hurt—and it wasn't likely to be the trainer. She got her father settled in the house, picked up her papers, and drove back to school, feeling numb.

Jace was struggling with a barbed-wire fence when he heard his cellular phone ring. He grudgingly took it out of his pocket and wiped the moisture sheening his face. "Yeah?"

"A fire at the Shelton ranch!" the dispatcher said.

"No!" Jace yelped.

"Just got the call. Everyone's gathering at the fire station."

"Send them out in the truck pronto. I'm on my way to the ranch."

"Sure thing."

Jace had been there only two nights ago when he'd driven Marla and all her birthday presents home. He dropped everything and ran to the pickup, slammed it into gear, and raced down the dirt road to the main highway.

When Jace arrived, swirling smoke lifted from the house's roof. His adrenaline pumping, he braked hard, the tires skidding on the gravel, and bolted from the pickup at a run. JoAnn Shelton emerged from the front door, coughing and holding her chest. "Charlie's trapped upstairs," she cried. "He slipped and I can't get him up."

Jace did a double take as something clicked in his mind. "What happened?" he asked.

"I don't know," she said, wringing her hands.

Then he spotted Hull wielding a hose by the kitchen. What was he doing here? The man tried to douse the flames that spread their molten fingers across the roof.

"Charlie!" JoAnn screeched. "Save him!"

Jeff came running up with another hose and attempted to water down the hot roof from a different angle. Jace started for the open front door.

"Everyone stay here," he called over his shoulder. "I'll get Charlie."

Jace strained to see beyond the thickness of the smoke, then hurled himself into the living room. He yanked the bandanna he wore from around his neck and tied the cloth bandit-style over his nose.

"Now where the heck is the master bedroom?" he grumbled, squinting.

Fumes temporarily disoriented Jace as a frightening epiphany hit him. The water heater could blow at any moment. That's all he needed. His mission was to save Charlie Shelton.

Jace forced other thoughts from his mind and took the steps two at a time. Without warning, a wall of smoke rolled down the staircase. He turned his back until it passed, then lunged up to the landing.

"Charlie!" he called.

No answer.

Jace stumbled along the corridor, taking quick glances inside bedrooms. Cursing fate, he sped on to the last room at the end of the hall. Charlie lay on the floor by the bed, his crutches propped up on a chair a few feet away.

"Jace!" he shouted. "Over here, son!"

Jace bent to help the man to his feet and flinched when Charlie groaned loudly. Jace heard a wrenching sound above in the ceiling and glanced upward. Timbers could soon give way. "We've got to get you downstairs," he said.

Charlie broke into a hacking cough, then said, "Can't get on them crutches, Jace. Hurt my ribs."

That meant picking Charlie up and carrying him down the staircase. Could Jace do it? Did he have an option? Then he saw orange-red flames lick through the ceiling, and bits of soot fell like hail.

Careful of Charlie's injured leg, Jace lifted the smaller man into his arms and lurched toward the door. A searing feeling in his lungs momentarily weakened him but he kept a firm hold on Charlie and started down the hall. Belching smoke burned his eyes.

Charlie grunted and tried to get to his feet, which made the burden even more difficult for Jace. "Be still," Jace growled.

He re-positioned his friend at the top of the stairs and began the perilous descent, taking one step at a time. Fearing Charlie would tumble forward if Jace stumbled, he said a short prayer.

The going got tougher as his vision worsened. Charlie felt like he weighed a ton. Jace was nearly on his knees when they broke through the entrance door into fresh air. Hacking, he carried Charlie across the yard to his pickup and laid the man on the truck bed. JoAnn Shelton raced to her husband, crying his name.

Marla ran up to Jace. He hadn't realized she was there. "Is Dad all right?" she asked in a terrified voice.

"I think so," Jace coughed, expelling smoke from his lungs. Marla pulled him toward her. "And you?"

"Okay, hon. Okay."

She looked relieved. The fire engine from Coyote Springs arrived, siren blaring, and swung into the yard. Everyone turned to look as the men unlatched hoses and raised a ladder. The fire continued to roll in bright orange and licks of blue up the kitchen side of the house.

"Thank the dear Lord they're here!" JoAnn cried. "This is awful."

Marla turned back to Jace and stared at his dark arms. "You're burned," she exclaimed. "Let me help you. I've got a first aid kit in the tack room."

"No need," Jace said.

He hurried to help the fire fighters. With determination, the men got the fire under control. Though the kitchen was gutted and the rooms above heavily damaged, the major section of the house was saved.

The fire fighters helped to clean up as best they could. "We'll need to wait until tomorrow to do much more," Jace said. "Everything's too hot." The men agreed.

Except for smoke inhalation, Charlie was in good shape, thanks to Jace. Although he'd bruised his ribcage in the fall, he refused to go to the hospital.

The happiest day of Marla's life was seeing Jace carry her father away from the burning house. She'd been terrified both men might perish. Could she ever thank Jace enough—her hero? He'd risked his life to save her father.

JoAnn turned to her daughter. "How do you think the fire got started?"

Marla shrugged her shoulders. "I wonder if we'll ever find out."

JoAnn shook her head. "You'd already left for school when I smelled smoke."

"Must have started in the kitchen," Jace said.

"Seems so," JoAnn said.

"Good thing Hull and Jeff were here to lend a hand," Jace added. "It at least gave the firemen a head start."

JoAnn glanced around. "I was surprised to see Hull. I guess he forgot something."

Marla shrugged. "It could have been an electrical fire, I suppose," she said, thinking of more important matters. "You hear about things like that happening in these old houses."

Everyone agreed. When the firemen rolled up the hoses and were about to leave, Charlie and JoAnn thanked the men profusely.

"No problem," they said in unison as they clamored aboard the fire engine. "We'll be here tomorrow and do more clean up work," the driver added. "See you then, folks."

"I'll be here, too. You can bet on it," Jace joined in.

"Thanks, Jace," Charlie said. "I'd been a goner without you."

Jace didn't know quite what to say, just tilted his soot-covered hat. "You all ought to come over and stay at the ranch with us for awhile," he suggested. "This place is pretty torn up."

"Thanks for the offer, but we'll be okay," Marla said.

Jace wished she wasn't always so all-fired independent. "I'm not letting you go back in that house until it's been checked out," he said firmly. "And I'm the fire chief."

"Oh, c'mon," Marla said. He shook his head. "All right, then, we'll sleep in the bunkhouse."

"I can lend you some of my ranch hands tomorrow," he volunteered.

"Take you up on it," Charles said. "The sooner this debris is cleared out, the sooner we can get our lives back to normal."

Marla looked around. "Where's Buck?" Her heart nearly stopped when she didn't see the puppy.

"I tied him in the barn," JoAnn said. "He was chasing the chickens again."

Marla felt better. She turned to Jace. He had red eyes, his hair scorched, along with his eyebrows. "I don't know what we would have done without you."

He slipped his arm around her waist and gave her a gentle hug. "Don't give it another thought, hon. Just glad I could help."

Marla knew she would always be indebted to him. She looked at his injured forearms. "I'm going to the tack room to get some clean dressings for those arms and don't give me any argument," she said. "Be right back."

"If you insist," Jace said, making light of the damage. He took a lawn chair and joined Charlie and JoAnn. They sat across from him in a glider swing, the damaged house an ugly backdrop behind them. "You okay, Charlie?" Jace asked. The older man looked too pale.

"Can't complain." Charlie glanced over his shoulder. "We were lucky the house didn't burn clean down to the ground. That fire was hot. Thank God you came along when you did, son."

JoAnn looked up at the house with misgivings. "I can't imagine how it got started. I know I didn't leave anything cooking on the stove."

Jace wiped his soot-stained hands on the thighs of his jeans. "I doubt the fire started by itself," he said, his voice tinged with skepticism. "From the looks of it, it must have started on the roof or in the attic."

"We should have gotten rid of that old furniture up there," Charlie said, swiveling his head toward his wife. "The mice probably made nests in it."

"I guess we'll never know what happened," JoAnn said with a shrug. "Jace, I'm so grateful you got Charlie down safely, but I hope you didn't hurt yourself, too."

"Naw," Jace assured her. He glanced around, expecting to see Marla come back.

Chapter Thirteen

Marla entered the subdued light of the stables. Horses whinnied and stuck their heads over the gates, their nerves heightened from smelling smoke. She called them by name in a reassuring tone as she walked along then opened the tack room door. Hull glanced up without speaking and slammed a battered briefcase shut.

"I didn't expect to find you here," she said, then saw a file drawer standing open.

He grunted. Marla figured he'd come for the papers he'd originally sent them and wondered why he didn't just ask for the file. She thought of confronting him, then let it slide. If he thought those papers were so important, so be it. She'd planned to toss them anyway.

Ignoring Hull, Marla crossed the room to the cabinet that contained first aid supplies and removed some items. His eyes followed her. Being alone with Hull made her feel uncomfortable. She glanced back at him. "Thanks for helping douse the flames," she said.

Hull flushed and looked down at his hands, then stared hard at her. "You folks didn't treat me right," he said through clenched teeth.

Marla sighed. "I'm not going to get into an argument with you now."

In the next moment Hull shifted his weight. Marla sensed danger and thought she ought to leave. She closed the cabinet and took a step toward the door.

Hull broke into a diabolic laugh that made her shudder and her mouth go dry. "What?" she stammered. Had he started the fire?

Hull glared at her. "So you figured it out, little lady. I see it on your face."

"I don't know what you mean."

The man took two strides across the room before Marla could react and grabbed her wrists, causing the ointment and bandages to fall on the floor.

"You're such a little idiot," he said with a sneer. "Why did you have to drive me away? I cared about you. We coulda' got rid of your old man and made something of this place."

Marla felt the outrage burn in her, a white-hot blaze that shot through her body. "Are you nuts?" she asked. He tightened his hold. "Let go, darn it!"

The trainer's features twisted oddly and his lips drew back in an uneven grin, revealing stained enamel. Marla's anger switched to fear. She hadn't been this scared since that Halloween night when she was five years old.

"We're getting out of here," he said, jerking her by the arm. "I've been watching you. I know you're not satisfied with the way things have been going, either."

Then he paused. "I never meant to burn the house down, just wanted to be a hero for once. Jeff and I coulda' got the fire out without that big cowboy and those firemen sticking their noses in."

Marla went cold. "Then you did set the fire? Oh, Hull, how could you?"

"Started it in an old overstuffed chair up in the attic when your ma was in the yard feeding the chickens."

Marla tried to wrench free. "Stop struggling," he demanded. "Let's get going. We can be in Mexico by dark."

"You can forget that idea!" she exclaimed, aiming a misguided kick at his shins.

Out of the corner of her eye, Marla saw Jace walk by the small window and she tried to distract Hull by struggling with all her worth. Then Jace was inside the door, Hull's back to him. Mouth clenched, Jace leaped across the floor, collared Hull and slammed a fist into his jaw before the man even knew what hit him.

Hull let go of Marla in a hurry and she ran behind Jace as he took another swing at the other man's nose. Blood spurted. Hull howled like a castrated bull and raised his fist. Jace twisted him around into a hammerlock. Marla tried to help but Jace yelled, "Get a rope."

She followed his order and tied the man's hands behind his back. All the fight had gone out of Hull and he slumped to the floor. Marla fell into Jace's arms. His smile reassured her.

Jeff came running, a shovel in his hands. "What the . . . ? You didn't come back, so I . . ."

Jace turned to him. "We have our culprit here," he said, sounding like Sherlock Holmes. "Meet the firebug."

Jeff glared at the trainer. Hull worked his jaw. His nose was still dribbling a little blood. "Durn fool," Jeff said.

"You shouldn't have gotten violent, Van Garrett," Hull said. "I intend to sue you for damages."

"Just try it," Jace said, his eyes darting menacingly at the man. "After you get out of jail, that is."

Marla stepped back into the circle of Jace's embrace and pressed her cheek against his chest, her body still reacting to the frightening experience. "Jace," she murmured, "Hull wanted me to go away with him. I can hardly believe it."

"I'll break his neck," he roared.

Marla loved Jace's strength, the way he'd come to her family's aid, and could scarcely believe how fast he'd ended her confrontation with Hull.

"He's not worth the bother," she said.

Jace turned to the man, his voice cold and metallic. "It took me a little while to figure it but I found out all about you," he said. "Got an interesting call last night. Then it hit me. You couldn't be in two places at the same time. Yeah, you copied your successful brother's resume and inserted your own name. That's fraud."

Hull glowered. "He won't press charges."

Jace ignored his comment. "The Shelton's may have trusted you in the beginning but I didn't from the get-go."

"You can't prove nothin'." Hull snorted.

Jace shook his head. "Oh, really? I have the report and the calls. After reading it, your whole sordid scheme glowed like a red neon sign. I was coming over after work to tell these folks, even though you'd left. Why, you've even served time." Hull glowered but Jace paid no attention. "You'll never be the man your brother is because you're a lazy, lying, good-for-nothing." He shook his head. "There's always temptation to do wrong. Apparently you prefer that route. Now you're going to take a little trip into town with Jeff and me."

Hull grumbled but could say little to deny the allegations. Marla stooped to pick up the things she'd dropped. Now she knew why he had stolen those papers. Jace and Jeff set the man roughly on his feet. Hull bristled. "I see you're one of them good guys who wear those white hats like some movie cowboy, Van Garrett," he said with disdain. "Probably have coffee with the sheriff down at the coffee shop every Sunday morning after church."

Jace tensed, his face molded granite. Marla put her hand on his shoulder. "Don't let him rile you," she cautioned.

To her relief, Jace backed off. "You're all that matters to me," he said to her with emotion. Their eyes locked in a tender embrace, then he turned to Jeff. "Let's take this turkey to see the sheriff."

Jeff's face lit up. "That was my thinking."

"Don't forget that briefcase. I think the sheriff will want to see it," Marla said.

Jeff picked it up and tucked it under his arm. Marla followed them from the tack room. Jace took a few moments to explain everything to the Sheltons. Then they put the prisoner in Jace's pickup and drove away from the ranch.

After he left, Marla realized she hadn't put bandages on Jace's arms. Why hadn't she made him take a few minutes? She glanced around at the devastation, but was glad the house still stood there.

Within an hour, Jace returned. Marla was clearing debris near the kitchen door. He stared down at her and slipped his arm around her waist in that familiar way he had, his gaze roaming over her face. The love she saw shining in the depths of his eyes nearly took her breath away.

"You're so beautiful," Jace said. She reached up and kissed his cheek. "I'd have skinned Hull if he'd harmed you."

Marla gave a soft sigh. "I can always count on you, Jace," she said with a tremor in her voice. "A million thanks, my love."

"Anytime, darling," he murmured and nuzzled the curve of her throat.

Marla thought about the wanna-be trainer languishing in jail. "I think Hull must have been stalking me. He admitted watching me. There were times when I felt I wasn't alone. It gave me an eerie feeling."

Jace's facial muscles tightened. "What do you mean?"

"Once in a while I could swear someone was watching me, but I never saw anyone."

Jace definitely didn't like hearing this and held her closer. "The guy was missing a few nuts and bolts in the brain department," he said. "Sounds like he could have been obsessed with you."

"I never gave him any encouragement," she said stoutly. "Why, I don't recall him even saying anything out of line. What a strange man!"

"Deranged people don't need much of a reason. They

imagine all sorts of weird things that aren't based on fact."

"I feel almost sorry for him."

"Don't bother your pretty head about Hull. He wasn't so crazy he didn't know right from wrong. He made those bad choices."

Marla nodded. "I want to forget he ever set foot on this ranch."

Jace gave her a long look. "I'm here to help you."

She tossed him a loving smile. "I feel better already, even if a heap of work lays ahead." Somehow her family would pull together and get through this, and she knew Jace and their friends would help. It had always been that way here in the valley.

Marla looked at Jace's forearms. "I still haven't put ointment on your arms. They look blistered."

"No need," he said.

"Don't be so darn stoic. Come on to the bunkhouse. We'll get you taken care of real quick."

Jace didn't move. Curious, she glanced up at him. He was giving her that intense "Jace" look again. "Okay," she said. "What gives?"

Then he said the words every girl in love wants to hear over and over. "I love you," he murmured, "and I'll always be around to protect you."

He kissed her with a warm sweet insistence that made every cell in her body glow. Then his lips teased the stem of her throat, her earlobes, her temples. His ardor intensified until she was weak with passion, her breath coming too fast.

Finally, Marla got hold of herself and pulled away.

"Whoa, cowboy," she cried, though she wanted these thrilling, intimate feelings to go on.

Jace stepped back and locked his eyes on her with such tenderness she almost threw her arms around his neck again. "It's your call, darlin'," he said with a sigh. "But I'd rather go on kissing you."

Marla contained a giggle. "The folks will want to talk to you."

Jace nodded. "Sure."

She took his hand and they strolled to the bunkhouse. JoAnn had Charlie comfortably settled on a cot, pillows propped behind his back. They gathered round him.

"I hoped you'd come back, Jace," Charlie said, his voice grittier than usual due to smoke inhalation. "I owe you one, big time. Say, what do you think made Hull do what he did?"

"It's hard to tell. Somewhere along the line he developed a mean plot to get even when you didn't buy his super-trainer act."

"Like burning the house down and killing us all in our beds," Charlie sputtered.

Jace took a breath and exhaled, as though getting rid of the terrible notion. "Maybe not actually kill you. Just scare the willies out of you. At least that's what he told the sheriff. Thought he'd put out the fire and be a hero, then you wouldn't make him leave."

Charlie shook his head. "He did that, all right—scare the willies out of us."

"Seems like he developed a distorted attachment for Marla, as well," Jace said with a frown. "Maybe that's when things started going haywire."

"I knew right off he wasn't much of a worker," Charlie said. "But I needed him too much by then to get rid of him."

Marla spoke. "I shouldn't have hired him, but with his good credentials, he seemed so right for the job."

"Don't beat yourself up," her father said. "You meant well."

Marla clutched her father's hand. "Dad, I don't even want to think of what could have happened."

"I'm still here, thanks to my soon-to-be son-in-law." Charlie grinned at Jace. Then his tone changed. "Hull's kind doesn't feel sorry for what they do, only that they don't get caught."

"Everything will be all right now," Jace said. "I'll get some of my boys out here first thing tomorrow morning to help clear off the burned parts. I wouldn't be surprised if some of the neighbors are already mobilizing."

The Sheltons were grateful. "Thanks, Jace," Marla said with a lump in her throat. So much had happened since she'd returned to the valley.

Jace gave her a warm smile. "You all get some rest now," he said.

Marla walked him to his truck. He embraced her then gave her a kiss that set her heart ablaze. "We haven't set a date for our marriage yet," he said out of the blue. "Have you thought about it, hon?"

"All the time, but I guess this isn't a good time to be thinking of that."

"Oh, but it is, darling. Let's say the day after your folk's house gets rebuilt. What do you think?"

"Perfect," she said. Then she dropped her voice. "Won't that take a long time?"

Jace grinned, and touched her lower lip with his

thumb. "I'll get the whole community out here tomorrow and we'll put that house together before you know it."

"By Christmas?"

"Before. We'll have a grand Christmas wedding right there in front of your fireplace, and we'll invite so many friends and relatives they'll be spilling out the doors."

Marla visualized herself in a white wedding gown standing proudly beside Jace. "Oh, I can't wait," she cried.

"Me, either, darling." Jace picked up her up and whirled her around, then gave her a tender kiss.